# A QUEST OF UNDOING

## BOOK ONE

JOHN P. LOGSDON

CHRISTOPHER P. YOUNG

**Published by**: Crimson Myth Press (www.CrimsonMyth.com)

**Edited by**: Lorelei J. Logsdon (www.LoreleiLogsdon.com)

**Cover art:** Jake T. Logsdon (www.JakeLogsdon.com) & Ric Lumb (www.PuttyCad.co.uk)

# COMMENTS

"Some of the funniest stuff I've ever read, and I've read some pretty funny stuff! I like that word: stuff."
—*John Logsdon*

"There are those who sayeth I scribed the basis of modern-drama. I don't knoweth about all thateth, but I wouldeth acknowlege that I penned a thrilling tale hereth and thereth. However, it musteth be saideth that I would joyfully undo all of my contributonseths if the resultant effect meanteth that these two hacketths were disallowed from ever writing again…eth."
—*William "Billy" Shakespeare*

"Billy spelled 'contributionseths' incorrectly."
—*Lorelei Logsdon*

"I have seen a sunrise gentle enough to bud the flower, yet strong enough to melt the soul. I have felt the loving caress of mother nature's balmy breeze and I have survived the ripping storms of her wrath. Prior to viewing this book, however, I never understood that for every work of wonder (such as, for example, *East of Eden*) there must live its antithesis. In case you're slow, I'm saying that this book is awful."
—*J. Steinbeck*

"Of all the books in my library, I come back time and time again to *A Quest of Undoing*. I just can't help myself because it's so cool that my name is on the cover!"
—*Chris Young*

"Read my son's book. He's a good boy."

—*Linda Logsdon*

# SENTENCING

*T*here he stood, like many before him, wondering what he'd done.

Charges against were kept secret until the day of the trial. It was one of the many staples of the Wizards' Guild, along with excessive drinking, lollygagging, and general avoidance of anything resembling work. Classifying allegations only served to ensure the accused had no time to do what wizards did best: think something up.

"It says here," said Councilwoman Muppy, the chair of the guild, "that Treneth of Dahl is accusing Master Xebdigon Whizzfiddle of never having successfully completed a quest."

"To the letter," Treneth amended.

"Hmmm?"

"I am accusing Master Whizzfiddle of never having successfully completed a quest to the letter of the contract."

Whizzfiddle plucked through the cobwebs of his memories. He assumed that somewhere along the vastness of his experience there rested at least one actualized contract. Unfortunately, nothing came to mind. He had learned at a

JOHN P. LOGSDON & CHRISTOPHER P. YOUNG

young age that people had little desire to continue with a dangerous adventure after the first couple of setbacks.

"I assume you have evidence of this?" Whizzfiddle said.

Treneth held up a folder and approached the bench. "These are all of the contracts that Whizzfiddle has been a party to over the last eleven hundred years. I have perused each of these contracts—"

"So you just glanced over them," Whizzfiddle interrupted, "and you put charges against me?"

"You need to find a dictionary, sir," Treneth answered with a snotty grin. "The term 'peruse' has been watered down through improper use over the years. Let's just say that I have carefully examined each contract and have found that not a single one has been done to the letter." He began pacing in front of the council members. "Now, you'll find no complaints on his record. All of his clients seemed pleased to work with the man. However," he said, stopping in front of Whizzfiddle, "according to the recent update to the Wizards' Guild membership requirements, each wizard must fulfill *all* obligations stated in a contract at least one in twenty times."

Whizzfiddle cleared his throat. "Then I shall do so effective immediately."

"A wise decision, were it available to you. You see, the legislation asseverates that it applies to the last one hundred quests."

"Preposterous!" Whizzfiddle declared, making a mental note to look up "asseverates," making a further note to find someone who could spell it.

"I wholeheartedly agree," Treneth replied in earnest.

"You do?"

"I do." Treneth sauntered back to the prosecution's chair. "I think we would all agree how preposterous—to use your term—it is that our longest tenured member has never finished a single quest properly."

Whizzfiddle scowled at the man's back. Always one for details was Treneth of Dahl. Cunning, cagey, crafty, and a slurry of other words that the elder wizard attributed to his former apprentice, most of which were ascribable to any wizard. But they seemed to fit extra well with Treneth. And now these descriptors were being used in a careful pursuit to get back at Whizzfiddle for releasing his former apprentice so many years ago.

The council set about debating.

After thirty minutes of waiting for the verdict, Whizzfiddle's legs began to cramp. It wasn't easy being perpetually old. He had been gifted this perpetuity of life by completing a Fate Quest that slowed his aging process to the point where one year for him was like one day to everyone else. If only this quest had been available to him when he was 50, life would have gone much more smoothly. Sadly, it didn't avail itself until he'd turned 650.

He retrieved his staff and decided to stroll around the council floor to stretch his muscles.

Whizzfiddle had sat on the council in the past, nearly half a lifetime ago. The room itself hadn't changed much over the years. It still had the high ceilings with the thick oak crossbeams. While it served as the Wizards' Guild chambers at certain hours, it was normally the home of Hibberton's School for Gifted Attiliators, which explained all of the crossbows and target boards, and the arrows that littered the floor. Originally, the guild had attempted affiliation with Hibberton's School for Crafty Cooks. Due to a speech impediment of the Hibberton's trust manager, where he had a tendency to make a "kw" sound for the letter "c," the Thieves' Guild had won the location. Still, Whizzfiddle reflected, their location turned out better than what the Sewing Club and the Farmer's Federation got: the Gong Farmer Academy and the Kipper's Cotters, respectively.

Finally, he went back to his chair and turned his focus on his former apprentice. Other than looking a couple hundred years older, Treneth was still as prim and proper as ever. If anything, the gray streaks in his thick helmet of hair made him look more dapper. Even the man's leather gloves had a nice shine to them.

The volume of the panel's debate gradually increased and laughter fell in with the discussion. Councilman Ibork, the grossly overweight halfling, tended to snort when he laughed; the Croomplatt twins, Councilman Elik and Esin—who appeared human, but nobody was one hundred percent certain of that fact—yelled the only word they could command in standard language, "ha," which could have many meanings depending on context, but happened to fall in perfectly with jovial pursuits; and even the elf, Councilman Zotrinder, the most vocally reserved member of the council, proffered a "heh heh."

"Madam Councilwoman," Treneth said after a time, "can I assume that the council has reached a decision?"

"Not quite," Muppy said as she adjusted her robe. "There are many options and this may take time."

"May I offer a suggestion?"

She pursed her lips. "Why not?"

"Very well," Treneth said, rising. "It is clear that you all have reservations about removing Whizzfiddle's membership, even if it is the right thing to do. Thus, I would suggest that you deem it necessary for the defendant to seek and contract a new quest promptly, say within the next twenty-four hours. He then must complete that contract *to the letter* within one month. Failure to comply or succeed to the fullest extent will result in immediate discharge from the guild."

Whizzfiddle saw a bunch of nodding heads and found he was nodding too. He stopped.

The council resumed their huddle for a few more moments.

"Yes," Muppy declared finally, "we'll do that."

# PREPARING FOR A QUEST

*W*hizzfiddle understood that quests were tedious things, so starting off correctly was paramount.

The problem was that Whizzfiddle had done so many over his years that he had grown bored with them. Doing magic was amazing, certainly, but the questing part of the gig was tiresome at best. There were too many details, they required tons of effort, and they took away time from life's most important enterprise: relaxation.

When it came to selecting quests, a wizard had to be choosy. Newer wizards grabbed after easier quests, as they were cheaper to hire, but established magic-doers tended to be a bit more cautious, carefully seeking different options with each new contract. After all, it was a rare wizard who wanted to be typecast.

Regardless, wizards were always in demand because there was a limited set of them.

Magic was an easy thing to command, but a difficult thing to start. There were no grid lines or runes or things of that nature in the world of Ononokin, so in order to get into the profession, one had to dedicate time to finding their particular magical essence. It literally came down to locating the power source that fueled each hopeful sorcerer, and everyone was different. Some toiled for years, working as an apprentice to a seasoned wizard, only to meet the finality of life while having never successfully fired off even the simplest of spells.

Whizzfiddle had been one of the lucky few. He'd happened upon his magical source the day his father took him to the pub for his adulthood celebration. Prior to that evening, it looked as though he would inherit the family farm, carrying the name Lenny Flepp for all his days. But that night the booze ignited a sizzling augury that all but flipped his eyelids inside out. He'd taken on a new name, found a master, and toiled to learn the ins and outs of his new profession so that he could get to a place where toiling was no longer necessary.

The beauty of each substance that became a wizard's fuel was the balance that kept them from becoming too powerful. There was no such thing as a single wizard that could go on about casting grievous levels of magic. They either couldn't get enough essence to manage it or they would overdose on it and become completely useless. If Whizzfiddle wanted to do a massive spell, for example, he'd have to drink a lot. That would make him drunk, which in turn would set his channeling into a slur of words, haphazard lightning bolts sizzling this way and that, and Whizzfiddle himself being chased by an agglomeration of bunny rabbits and geese. He never quite understood what caused the rabbits and geese.

And that was how the world managed to keep wizards from having too much potency.

Having alcohol as one's magical essence was far better than what many wizards ended up with. One poor lad learned during a duel that his magical essence came from being stabbed in the heart. His wizarding life lasted only moments. There was one lady living in Argan who had to hang from a tree limb with her right hand only. This made swinging her wand around somewhat clumsy since she wasn't left-handed.

Whizzfiddle recalled the day that his former apprentice uncovered his particular source. They were walking the fields when an obstinate ostrich of some size took to chasing Treneth around. Being less than an athlete, the young man was no match for the speedy bird. Whizzfiddle had yelled for Treneth to lie down before the beast smashed him. Treneth kept turning this way and that to avoid dropping to the earth. He was far too prim and proper to subjugate himself to such an act. But he was tiring and the bird began pecking at the back of his head. Finally, which he later insisted was due to a trip and not an intentional act, Treneth dropped and slid face down into a mixture of mud and ostrich feces. The concoction slipped under his fingernails and his power was born. Whizzfiddle still cringed at what his apprentice had done to that poor bird.

The elderly wizard sighed as he strolled through the town of Rangmoon toward Gilly's Pub, his place of operation.

Gilly's stood near the center of the bustling streets in his beloved city. It wasn't much to look at. The roof shingles had been laid out in a haphazard pattern that made one wonder how many buckets were needed inside during a rainstorm. Most of the windows were either cracked, dulled, or both, and the frames were rotted. The siding had all but lost its most current painting, which, if Whizzfiddle's eyes weren't fooling him and his memory served, was a yellowish-reddish-bluish color. The building's only redeeming quality was being situated between Furnitureland and the town's clothier, A Hint of Moon, a shop known for its somewhat transparent garb.

JOHN P. LOGSDON & CHRISTOPHER P. YOUNG

But Gilly's had the finest ale in all of the land. To a wizard whose livelihood depended on liquor, fine ale was more important than looks.

The familiar stench of stew and soured booze filled the air as Whizzfiddle pushed through the main door of Gilly's Pub and headed purposefully toward the back.

He stopped at the decorative rail that bordered a lofted platform where a single table sat in the corner. It was Whizzfiddle's table. Not just a favorite table. No, he had paid for it when the original pub had opened many generations of Gillys ago. It had cost him a good deal to ensure that the table would be cleared for him whenever he entered the establishment and he still paid a yearly fee to maintain that right.

It had been quite a while since his last visit to Gilly's. He only attended for quest-seeking, quest-preparation, and post-quest celebrations.

A part of him wished he had selected a different pub for wizarding purposes. He much preferred Gilly's ale to Libertin's Tavern or the horrendously bad Cuts & Ale Depot, but those places had more pizazz.

He shrugged, rubbed his hands together, and stepped up into his "office."

As was his custom, he knelt to take a look under the table. *"Whizzfiddle was here"* was engraved above the series of lines that indicated how many quests he had sought over the years. After getting to twenty-five he lost interest in the count and instead set about carving in a new line.

"Master Whizzfiddle, sir," said a familiar voice.

Whizzfiddle peered up and gave a quick nod to the greasy-haired pub owner, then resumed his work under the table.

"'Tis a right pleasure seeing you again," Gilly said. "I was just tellin' the wife not two days back how we'd not seen Master Whizzfiddle for quite a spell."

Whizzfiddle held up a finger to convey he needed a moment. He heard Gilly grunt and then watched the man spin and storm off, his boots pounding the rickety wood floors with each step.

Whizzfiddle paused his carving. He retraced the scene, unveiling that his attempt to convey pause had yet again failed.

It never ceased to amaze the elderly wizard how significantly one's communicative intent was changed by holding up the wrong finger.

## TRENETH OF DAHL

*T*reneth preferred his office to be free of color and playfulness.

Heavy brown curtains surrounded a lone window that allowed a speck of light to peek through. Lanterns offered plenty of visibility for his tidings and Treneth kept them running at full both day and night. His diplomas, awards, and accolades were all set in perfect alignment to the wooden planks that ran from floor to ceiling. Each frame was made of the same dark mahogany as the paneling.

He scanned the room as he always did, seeking for anything out of place.

Satisfied that all was in order, he stepped into the room. He was careful to avoid the third floorboard. It always creaked. Creaking was a sign of imperfection. Treneth abhorred imperfection. He had learned to tolerate it because the world was full of it, but where it could be avoided he endeavored to do so. Repairing the board was not a priority in the grand scheme of things, and the dust, noise, mess, and disruption the fix would cause was out of the question.

He stopped at his large mahogany desk, noticing a

problem. He pointed to a smudge that sat just under the lip of its edge.

"Vigilance, Rimpertuz," Treneth said to his apprentice. "It is the only way we attain perfection."

Rimpertuz hustled over to buff out the smudge, stepping on the loose board and apologizing as he had done many times.

Treneth sighed.

A verbal lashing was almost always in order for Rimpertuz. Treneth had all but given up on trying to correct the man. As his father had once said, "You cannot make a diamond out of a piece of coal." It wasn't at all accurate, but the intended point was taken. Treneth had often toyed with the idea of dismissing Rimpertuz, but being linked to losing an apprentice would be another tarnish on Treneth's record. And, to be fair, Rimpertuz did have his uses now and then, being that he was just a cut above dimwit.

It was a good sign that the outbox sat reasonably higher than the inbox. He tidied up one of the stacks as he sat in his high-backed leather chair.

There was much work to be done. His aim was first a council seat and then the council chair.

Whizzfiddle's demise was an important step in attaining that goal because Treneth deplored unfinished business. It muddled his thinking. Since Whizzfiddle had a history of ignoring rules, or rewriting them, all Treneth had to worry about was setting things in motion and occasionally tweaking dynamics to keep his former master tripping.

Fortunately, the Wizards' Guild council had ruled in Treneth's favor, setting Whizzfiddle to have to complete a quest to the letter within thirty days. Knowing the old coot as he did, Treneth felt confident that the man's wizarding days were at a close. Vengeance was a beautiful thing, when done correctly.

"I have a special assignment for you, Rimpertuz."

"Yes, sir?"

"You will follow Master Whizzfiddle today and report to me any information that you glean." Treneth adjusted one of his pens to set it parallel to another. "We need to understand our prey. Do you understand?"

"Yes, sir," Rimpertuz said. "Which god are we praying to, sir?"

"No, Rimpertuz." Treneth closed his eyes and clicked his teeth. "Not *pray* as in seeking divine guidance—something we have discussed at length and, again, I will state that there is nothing divine to offer any such prayer to—p*rey* as in a rabbit to a fox."

"Yes, sir. Sorry, sir."

"Vigilance, Rimpertuz. Always. Now, you will find Whizzfiddle at that wretched pub by the clothier."

"Gilly's, sir," said Rimpertuz a little too quickly.

"Yes," he said at length while tapping a gloved finger on the desk. "You may frequent the establishment for this purpose only. I repeat, for this purpose *only*. Are we clear?"

"Yes, sir. I wouldn't dream of attending without your express permission, sir."

"Pray you do not."

"Like a rabbit to a fox, sir."

"No..." Treneth started and then shook his head. "Look, go to the pub and find out what you can, and keep yourself from being noticed."

"You can count on me, sir."

Sadly, Treneth could not. Treneth could only be in one place at a time, though, so Rimpertuz would have to do.

A thought occurred to him as Rimpertuz was shutting the door.

"One more thing! Keep a close eye on Whizzfiddle's hat. As long as I've known the man he's been hiding something under that hat and I would be quite pleased to learn what it is."

Now that his plan for Whizzfiddle's demise was flowing, he would have to think of how best to finagle his way on to the council.

Chairperson Muppy could be a formidable foe, but she was flighty at best. She had a temper, to be sure, and she had moments of clarity that Treneth would have to watch out for, but all in all he felt certain that she wouldn't be much of a deterrent to his goals; Councilman Ibork was an exceedingly fat halfling that was too much of a dullard to be of any real concern. He was more of a threat to a bowl of stew than to the likes of Treneth of Dahl; Councilman Zotrinder was an elf that was entirely too caught up in his looks and personal grooming regimen to even know what was going on half the time; and the Croomplatt twins, Elik and Esin, didn't have enough grasp of the local language to bring arguments against him regardless of what he did. They merely said "Ha!" as a response to most everything, and typically in unison.

Still, Treneth would have to be patient and smoothly set plans in motion so that he could ensure his spot on the council. Once that was complete, he would begin the next phase of taking over the main chair. Then he would be able to enact the rules and regulations that he believed every wizard worthy of the title should follow.

He leaned back and smiled.

Finally things were moving in the right direction.

## APPLICANTS

*A*s Gilly thumped back carrying ale, his expression seemed to be on the mend.

Whizzfiddle, not one for lengthy apologies, explained the misunderstanding and began draining the contents of his mug.

"Not to worry, sir." Gilly smiled, revealing more gums than teeth. "Any other gent would have been shown the door, but you've been a regular at this pub since my great-grandfather brewed his first batch."

"Yes," Whizzfiddle mused, noting to himself that it was *this* Gilly's great-great-great-and-so-on grandfather. Many generations had passed since Gilly's got its start. "I recall the day, in fact. Horrible excuse for a draft, that first batch."

He winked and wiped his mustache. It had taken the first Gilly months to relax enough to stop turning the malt to flour, and another few to get the perfect mixture of barley, hops, and a few secret ingredients before he could stake claim to the finest ale in the land.

Whizzfiddle lifted his mug and said, "Praise The Twelve that the Gillys are a tenacious lot."

"Aye, sir," Gilly beamed and then nodded at the window. "It looks like they're lining up already, sir."

Whizzfiddle sighed.

The line of would-be questing parties was slipping out to the middle of the road as the sun cleared its midway stroll.

One of the benefits of being the most experienced wizard in Ononokin was that you were always in demand. It left little in the way of anonymity, of course, but fame went with the territory and it was unquestionably better than farming for a living.

"I suppose two years of slumber is enough. Time to get on with it." He rapped on the table twice. "One more pint, if you please, and then you can start sending them in."

"As you say, sir."

"Oh, and Gilly, please do keep the ale coming at a reasonable pace."

## THE PRINCE

The first man to step up was adorned in a rich blue fabric with cuts so precise they marked the work of the finest artisan. Gold linings etched a tunic in a class by itself, and the many bits of dangling medallions fixed the man's status. His hair was golden blond and hung precisely past his shoulders. His beard was trimmed, framing his face and setting his bright blue eyes to shine.

"Prince?" Whizzfiddle asked as he dug his nail into the top of the table, careful to avoid another splinter.

"I…well, yes," the man replied.

"Kingdom in trouble?"

"No."

"Special assignment to demonstrate fealty?"

"No, that was last year," said the prince. "I succeeded quite nicely."

Whizzfiddle harrumphed. "Princess or princess-to-be—" He paused and looked over the prince again, and squinted while chewing at the inside of his cheek. "Or maybe prince?"

The man ruffled and grimaced.

"Right, right." Whizzfiddle smiled apologetically. "Never know these days, especially in an outfit like that."

The prince looked down at himself with a confused expression. "What's wrong with my outfit?"

"Nothing's *wrong* with it," said Whizzfiddle. "It's a dandy ensemble. Dandy indeed. What with the gold and all those jinglies. Immaculately detailed, to be sure."

The prince crossed his massive arms and glared at the elderly wizard.

"It's just a little, shall we say...elfish?"

Leaning forward, the prince pressed his hands on the table and said, "Can we get on with the interview, sir?"

Whizzfiddle felt the air simmering as the prince's cologne drifted toward him. It smelled of roses. He wasn't shocked.

"Yes, well, I'm assuming that you have a damsel in distress then?"

"Correct." The prince pushed off the table. "It has been over a week since we last heard anything."

Gilly had dropped off another tankard and Whizzfiddle drained its contents.

"Not to worry, lad," said Whizzfiddle. "She'll be fine."

The prince brightened. "Then you will assist my kingdom in its time of need?"

"I could," Whizzfiddle answered. He thought about how he would carry out the quest to the letter of the contract. He'd never succeeded at one of these quests in a spotless manner before, so it was doubtful he'd do so now. "Alas, I shall not."

"But they'll kill her."

"No, they won't. It's a game they play." Whizzfiddle adjusted his over-sized bottom to fit more snugly in the chair. "They'll have a little fun with her..." He looked up into those steel blue eyes and trembled. "What I mean is that they'll have a little fun trying to garner a ransom for her safe return."

"This note"—the prince pulled forth a folded piece of parchment—"says that if they don't receive the money within a fortnight her life will be forfeit."

"A fortnight?"

"Yes, that's what it says."

"Never quite understood the concept of a fortnight." Whizzfiddle pulled his foot up and itched it. "Damn vampires," he said, scratching a little red bump.

"You think that vampires took my love?" the prince said, horrified.

"What?" Whizzfiddle kept scratching. "No, I'm talking about these bumps. Look at them all."

His legs were covered with tiny red blisters.

"You mean mosquitoes."

Whizzfiddle often forgot that the people in the Upperworld were unaware of the people in the Underworld. The Upperworlders called the bugs that sucked blood "mosquitoes" or "those little bastards." But a prince should know about such things.

Whizzfiddle coughed.

"Yes, yes," he said, rubbing his leg on the chair. "Figure of speech, you know. What land are you from again?"

"Zerbaus. Does that matter?"

"Just wondering," Whizzfiddle answered, trying to recall the place. It didn't come to mind. "Is this a new—"

"It's been three years now. My father conquered the land between Argan and the Kesper's Range."

"Conquered, you say?" Whizzfiddle stuck a finger in his ear and pulled forth a bit of wax. He noted the prince had a look of disgust and so he wiped his finger under the table. "I don't recall there being anything to conquer between Argan and Kesper's."

"Well, no, not exactly."

"Last I remember it was overrun with wild sheep."

"And rabbits," the prince said with a huff.

"Rabbits," Whizzfiddle nodded. "I would imagine they put up quite a resistance to your invading forces."

"They're tougher than you know. They have big teeth!"

Whizzfiddle had never run into a rabbit that he couldn't skin. Sheep could be tricky if they all pulled together, but he'd only seen that happen once and there was magic involved.

"No portal then?"

"Portal?"

"To the Underworld."

"The what?"

"Hmmm. What were you before your father conquered the land of sheep and rabbits?"

The prince looked around the room and then back at Whizzfiddle. "A tailor."

"Ah," Whizzfiddle said, feeling a little bad. "That explains it."

If this land of Zerbaus was only a few years old, it would be too new to be on the map. It had probably not even been granted a deed as yet. Until it was a recognized land, the ruling class would not be privy to the Underworld or its workings. There may have been a few official knights, or ex-knights, as the case may be, that were aware of the realities of Ononokin, but they were sworn to secrecy. It was determined by the powers-that-be-who-are-long-since-dead that the Underworld should remain one of those need-to-know pieces of information. For now, the old statute stuck.

"Can we get back to the subject of the princess, please?"

"She'll be fine," said Whizzfiddle absently. "She'll likely even learn a few tricks you'll be glad of."

"Like what?"

"Erm, well, survival things, of course." He stood up and gestured toward the door. "Lad, she'll be fine, but you'll still need to find a wizard to assist you. Head down to Felatina's Felines, by the docks."

"Isn't that a gentleman's club?"

"I wouldn't classify it precisely that way, but that's close enough. You're looking for a man known as Varmint the Virile. Just call out his name and give him a moment before approaching since he'll probably be feeding the chickens, in a manner of speaking."

"I'm not sure I understand."

"You don't want to understand," Whizzfiddle said, directing the prince toward the door. "Just know that he adores these princess quests and he'll be so, um, concerned over the princess's psychological wellbeing after going through such a traumatic event that he'll insist on having a private audience with her multiple times a year for years to come."

## THE RING

*T*he next party consisted of a ranger, a soldier, an elf, a dwarf, and four hobbits. The smallest hobbit had curly black hair and bright blue eyes. He stepped forward and began opening his hand.

Whizzfiddle looked at the hand as it opened. He saw the dramatic nature of the creature, and figured he'd have time to finish his ale. Everyone else continued gazing in awe at the dreadfully slow halfling. Maybe the lad was suffering from arthritis or some similar ailment. Whizzfiddle didn't know, but he tapped his foot and signaled Gilly for another ale.

"Does it always take this long for the lad to open his hand?" Whizzfiddle whispered to the ranger.

The ranger replied with a frown.

By the time Gilly arrived, the little fellow had his hand opened enough that Whizzfiddle could spot a glowing golden ring that sported elvish writing.

"No, no, no." Whizzfiddle stood up, waving all about. "No! I do not do ring quests. Ghastly things, ring quests. Boring to no end. So many twists and turns. Pits of doom, betrayal, creepy little gray creatures that talk to themselves…and don't even get me started on the giant psychotic spiders."

All eyes were upon him, even other patrons in the pub. A scrawny man at another table had spilled a bit of stew down his shirt and was casting an angry eye toward the wizard.

The little blue-eyed halfling snapped his hand shut.

Whizzfiddle pointed at the door.

"Go down to Fourth and Buchanan, Yebberton's BBQ. Ask for a wizard named Gimdolf, Grimdoof, or Gamdorf? … or maybe it's Ginderolf? I suppose it could've been Geldof the Pink, too." He fished around in his brain, seeking the proper name. "Something like that," he said finally. "Just yell out that you have a ring quest and he'll pipe up. The man just loves these ring quests. Has a few books that he reads over and again and jumps at every opportunity for an adventure or even just idle debate on the topic."

Thanks were shared as the troop bolted out the door.

## THE FREAKS

*H*ours passed. Each filled with scores of people looking for help with ring quests, princess-in-distress quests, fealty quests, lost-throne quests, and every other cliché picking from the crop.

Whizzfiddle was ready to call it a day when Gilly told him that there was only one batch of adventurers left. He slouched back in his chair and waited for them to step up.

The old wizard's eyes lit up.

Before him stood a haggard and scrawny-looking knight, an overweight elf with severe acne, a seven-foot dwarf who somehow remained proportionate, and a four-foot-tall giant that was so squished down the wizard thought surely the fellow had been stepped on by a dragon and then stung by a hundred bees.

No rings, no hobbits, and no princes (or princesses).

"I don't care what it is," said Whizzfiddle, slamming back the remaining ale and smacking his lips. "I'll take it!"

# CHANGELINGS

hizzfiddle studied each of them for a moment. They had all been transfigured, which sometimes happened in battle. Take the most important people on the field, do a little hocus-pocus on them to mix up their physical and/or emotional attributes, and watch all their minions lose interest in continuing the battle. The change could be permanent or at least take years to wear off, with permanence coming about because the victim gradually begins to identify with the changes. Once it becomes an identity, it sticks.

And that was the challenge.

"Let us start with you, elf," Whizzfiddle said.

"I was once tall and lean, with golden hair as fair as the sun," the elf said, his voice quivering. "My eyes shone like emeralds set delicately within the purest of complexions."

Whizzfiddle leaned over toward the little giant. "Speaks like an elf," he whispered.

The elf exhaled. "Do you wish to hear of me or not?"

"Now, now," said Whizzfiddle with a squint. "I've not asked you to recant your life's tale, lad. There's no doubt you still have the spirit of an elf, even if the shell that carries it is without its typical splendor." The elf raised his nose at the remark. "Let us begin with your name."

"Orophin Telemnar," he replied, as though it were a song.

Whizzfiddle furrowed his brow and sat back, dragging the ale to his lips. It was a name that should be common among the elves, but the wizard had never heard it before.

"You know the meaning of this name, I assume?"

"Of course I do!" Orophin said. "Unlike most of my kind, the people in my village are allowed to choose the names of their children. The parents participate, to be certain, but the final name is decided by committee. They do so when the child becomes a young adult. Until then he is called with a temporary name." He scratched at a pimple that was near the point of bursting. "Apparently, the people in my village thought it would be funny to give the name to me. Little did they know that I would one day become their prince!"

The others shook their heads, faces back in their respective steins, except for the tiny giant.

He looked at Whizzfiddle. "What it mean, mister?"

Whizzfiddle ignored the question. "Prince, eh?" he said to the elf. "I don't recall any elf prince named Orophin."

"Nor would you have. I was removed as speedily as I was elected. It was clear that whoever ended up as the next prince would be targeted by our adversaries, so they moved me into that position."

"Who made you prince?" asked Whizzfiddle.

"The elders, of course," Orophin replied. "It was a glorious day for me." He smiled briefly before his face drooped. "Since that day it has been the nightmare that you see before you. I doubt that I'm even a footnote in elvish lore at this point."

"Why do you expect they made you prince?"

"Because they wanted to do away with me, obviously!"

"Obviously," agreed the wizard. "But *why* did they want to do away with you?"

"Because I'm…well…it's that I'm—"

"Gay," the others chorused, finishing Orophin's sentence.

The elf bit his lower lip and closed his eyes.

Whizzfiddle searched his memories for any incident whereby an elven community had persecuted one of its own for such a petty reason. Now, if Orophin had declared himself straight that would be another matter entirely.

"I don't understand why this would be a problem."

"Well, being different is not something that the elves endure well."

"True," Whizzfiddle said. "They don't at that, but what does being gay have to do with being different?"

"I'm different *because* I'm gay."

"What?" Whizzfiddle roared. "I thought all elves were gay!"

After a few moments the room had settled down. The only two who had not taken part in the merriment of the comment were Orophin and Whizzfiddle; the former because of the obvious, the latter because he was sincerely confused by the statement made by the former.

"Think about it, wizard," Orophin said through gritted teeth. "If all elves were gay, how would we have children?"

Whizzfiddle opened his mouth to reply, but stopped.

"Actually," he said, stroking his beard, "I've never considered the point."

"And do you think all female elves are lesbians as well?"

"Heavens, no," Whizzfiddle replied as if slapped.

"Praise The Twelve," the enormous dwarf agreed.

"Anyway," Orophin said, "there you have it. I was given my name by my people, made prince to take a horrific fall, and then condemned into a body that no self-respecting, half-attractive man would want to love."

31

They were all quiet now.

"Mister?" The giant tugged on the wizard's sleeve.

"Yes, little friend?"

"What the name mean?"

"Ah," Whizzfiddle said, tipping his ale again. "I believe that you will need to ask the elf that question."

"He not answer when I talk to him."

It meant "the gay elf of Telemnar," but Whizzfiddle didn't see it as his place to share that information.

The wizard looked around the table, settling back on the dinky giant. The midget looked quite odd because he was so huge for a little man. He was like a hobbit that had gone a little overboard at the buffet...for the past twenty years. His hair was a bushy brown that matched the color of his deep-set eyes. His teeth were crooked, where there were teeth. His hands were abnormally large compared to his frame, so much so that Whizzfiddle guessed the runt could crush a dragon's windpipe without a thought.

"What of you, little giant?" The response was simply an odd and confused look. "Right, right," Whizzfiddle said, patting him on his noggin. "Tell me your name and story!"

"Oh," the mini giant responded with a bit of snort. "I are Gungren, mister."

"Gungren?"

"That it, yep."

"Gungren," Whizzfiddle said while scratching the table, "tell me how you came to be such a wee lad."

"I were big before."

"Yes, I would imagine you were rather large indeed."

"That right," Gungren said with a sigh. "Until that wizard did a spell on me when I weren't lookin'."

"Were you a prince as well, my young Gungren?"

"I not young," Gungren said. "I nearly eighty summers. I just look young 'cause I small."

32

"Ah, indeed." Whizzfiddle tipped his hat. "Yet, were you a prince or king of your people?"

"No," he replied. "I were the muscle for the elf attack."

"I see," Whizzfiddle said, glancing over at Orophin for confirmation.

Whizzfiddle again studied the group. "Okay, so you were all part of the elf's party when a wizard jumped in and rearranged your anatomy."

"No," the knight replied. "Well, not precisely."

"Oh," Whizzfiddle said. "Please do tell."

"I am Knight Zelbaldian Riddenhaur of the Queen's Guard…" he stumbled, "…or I should say that I *was* a knight of the Queen's Guard. Now, I am simply Zel."

"Zel," Whizzfiddle affirmed.

"We were attacking with the elves," Zel continued. "I was leading the charge."

"Who were you attacking?"

"Ikas," said Orophin. "They have been expanding deeper into our forests and we finally had to put a stop to it."

"I thought the Ikas had given up their warring ways some years ago?" said Whizzfiddle.

Zel shrugged. "Apparently not. The point is that I was not only changed physically, but mentally as well."

"Aye," the large dwarf said. "That's what that bastard wizard did to me as well."

Even sitting down, Whizzfiddle had to crane his neck a bit. "And you are?"

"Bekner Axehammer."

"That's an odd name."

"I was equally skilled with both the axe and the hammer," Bekner explained.

"But why not Hammeraxe then?"

"Thought about it," the towering dwarf replied. "Just ain't got that ring that Axehammer has, ya see?"

33

"Matter of taste, I suppose."

Bekner clasped his hands. "Only matters how it tastes to the one wearin' it, as I see it."

It got quiet for a moment.

"Hammeraxe sounds more manly," Orophin said meekly.

"Are ye questionin' my manliness, elf?"

"Oh, no." Orophin waved his hands. "I've seen your manliness and there's no questioning that thing."

It got quieter than before.

"It's me, then?" Bekner had a look of horror on his face.

Whizzfiddle looked around the table, seeing a mix of hopeful expressions and one terrified gigantic dwarf.

"I'm still not telling," Orophin replied with an exasperated sigh.

"What's he talking about?"

Gungren said, "Orphan think one of us is cute and we not like that."

"Ah, I see."

"It's *Orophin*, you bulbous midget. O-R-O-P-H-I-N! Not Orphan!" He turned back to Whizzfiddle. "And I swore that until this was done that I would not tell who it was that I found suiting to my taste."

"I'll bet it's the knight," Whizzfiddle said, receiving stern glares from both Zel and Orophin. "What? You've got a dwarf, a giant, and a knight. Do the math, people!"

"Your math would be wrong," Orophin said with disdain, causing two groans and one sigh of relief.

"Interesting," Whizzfiddle said and then waved Gilly over and ordered another round, which Orophin refused, instead asking for water with lemon.

The pub was now teeming with patrons. Whizzfiddle was never one for crowds, and especially not one for noise, but that's what always happened as an evening progressed in a Rangmoonian tavern.

"Well," Bekner piped in, "you said you'd be after helpin' us."

"And help I shall."

"We have little in the way of payment," Orophin mumbled.

"I have little need of money," said Whizzfiddle. "I have need of an adventure to satisfy a guild requirement due to a..." He trailed off. His head was spinning and he shut his mouth. Something deep inside told him not to say too much just yet. "I won't waste time with details. Let's just say that I have to finish a quest in thirty days as part of a guild requirement, so if we work as a team we can have a mutually successful outcome."

"How does this work, then?" Zel asked.

"Simple enough. We have to find the wizard that did this to you and have him undo it."

"We know who it was," Orophin said.

"Aye, the rangy bastard," Bekner said.

Whizzfiddle wiped his beard and said, "As do I."

"You do?" Gungren asked.

"Lads," Whizzfiddle said with his hands out in grandiose fashion, "you don't get to be the level of wizard I am without knowing all there is to know about the world!"

"Hmmph," Orophin said. "You thought all elves were gay."

"Fair point," the wizard said with a nod, "but you probably think that all wizards are horribly selfish individuals who hold little regard for anyone or anything but themselves. No?"

There was no response.

"That's what I thought. Well, I'll tell you that it's not the case. Many of us are far worse than you'd expect." It was meant to be a joke, but they seemed to accept the comment at face value. "It was Peapod Pecklesworthy."

Astonished nods all around.

JOHN P. LOGSDON & CHRISTOPHER P. YOUNG

"Simple deduction, lads," Whizzfiddle said. "There aren't that many wizards in the Upperwo...um, north capable of managing transfigurations."

He pushed away from the table and stretched his arms.

"Well, then," he said after a full yawn, "I shall return to my home and prepare for the journey ahead. Get your supplies and make ready for an adventure. It will be challenging at times, so be primed for the worst!"

"It can't possibly get much worse," Orophin groaned.

"Actually, elf," Whizzfiddle said, "it can."

## AN APPRENTICE REPORTS

*T*he sun was just dipping past the horizon when Treneth saw Rimpertuz enter the garden. His apprentice's step was a little off kilter and his clothing was hanging on him haphazardly.

Treneth set his cup of tea on the counter and pushed through the screen door. The smell of ostrich was thick in the air. It was a smell that Treneth had come to appreciate because of the power their ejecta afforded him. Not only did it allow magic to flow through his veins, it also served as a wonderful fertilizer.

He stood on the landing as Rimpertuz continued staggering through the courtyard. The man was whistling and singing an old tavern song that Treneth hated. "The Ale of Glinderdoom." Treneth had many recollections of his father waking the house with that tune in the middle of the night.

Treneth feigned a cough.

"What have you learned, Rimpertuz?"

"Sir Treneth of *Dull*," Rimpertuz slurred and snickered, and then saluted. "Master Whizzer found a quest, sir!"

Treneth nearly gagged from the stench of alcohol. It was so strong that he held his gloved hand over his nose in order to smell the ostriches again.

It was grounds for dismissal. Alcohol of any sort was not tolerated in Treneth's realm, except as a disinfectant, what with ostriches and all. Were Rimpertuz not a pawn in his plans, Treneth would have terminated him on the spot. For now, this lapse in judgment would prove useful.

"What is the quest?" Treneth asked.

"As to that, it's a bunch of wom...wom...weirdies that don't look like they ought to look."

Rimpertuz swayed for a moment, looking a bit pale.

"Why don't you have a seat," Treneth said. "Now, tell me the entire story. Slowly, if you would."

"The dwarf was huge," Rimpertuz said, as if that explained everything.

"I will require more detail, Rimpertuz. Please start from the beginning."

"Okay," Rimpertuz said. "There was a lot of different opportun...opportun—"

"Opportunities."

"—options for quests. Even some simple types like princessesses and stuff. But he stuck fast to his wands and way...way...waited for something interesting to me."

"To you?"

"What?" Rimpertuz said.

"You said that Master Whizzfiddle waited for something interesting to you."

"I did?"

Treneth bristled, took a deep breath, and sighed. "Let us continue, Rimpertuz."

Rimpertuz attempted to cross his legs but kept missing. He grunted.

"So's as I was saying, it took all day and the food kept coming and so did the drunks...dranks...well, you know."

"Yes," Treneth said with a slight edge. "I *do* know."

"Super," the apprentice said with a mild sneer. "As Whizzy was about to walk out, these four fella's sho...show up and they were all weirdies."

"What precisely do you mean that they were weirdies?"

"Well, you know, they didn't loo...look right."

"Rimpertuz, this is important. I need you to concentrate. What can you tell me about the people that Master Whizzfiddle interviewed?"

"The dwarf was big. Real big."

"So you said earlier, yes."

"Yep, and he was standing next to a fat elf."

"A fat elf."

Rimpertuz winked and nodded. "There was a little guy there, but he was big really. Just not like he was."

"Explain."

"He was supposed to be a giant," Rimpertuz said.

"Are you certain that the dwarf wasn't the small one and that what you thought was a large dwarf was actually a giant?"

"I know what you mean, man," Rimpertuz said. "It confused the helloutta me too. But they were...was...were like I said."

"Wait," Treneth said, sitting back. "Are you saying that this is a Quest of Undoing?"

Rimpertuz grinned and clapped. "That's the one."

That was odd. It was one of the more challenging of quests. On the other hand, it *could* also be the simplest if Whizzfiddle knew who the responsible wizard was, and if that wizard owed a debt. As undisciplined as he was, Whizzfiddle knew how to play the system. Maybe Whizzfiddle wanted to go out in style, or maybe the old coot had been a bit too drunk to realize what he had gotten himself into.

"Did you get the name of the wizard that caused the transfiguration?"

"Yep."

Treneth clenched his teeth, but kept his cool.

"Could you give me the name, please?"

"I could," Rimpertuz said, "but I think we have to have a har...heart-to-heart chat first."

"Oh?" Treneth said, raising his eyebrow. "What would that be about, my dear *apprentice*?"

"I caught how you just said that wor...wor—"

"Word. And I'm glad you're of clear enough mind to have caught that."

"Listen here, fella," Rimpertuz said as he attempted to stand up. "I don't need to listen to you anymore, I think."

"Rimpertuz," Treneth said, "let me provide you some advice."

"No, no," Rimpertuz said, waving a finger. "I have something to say and it'll be good for you...me...us to hear it."

Treneth sat back as his apprentice managed to stand upright. After a few moments, the man spun around and seemed happy that he had found his master again. Then his eyes rolled up into his head and he keeled over.

As Rimpertuz snored, Treneth thought of wizards in the region that were capable of transfigurations.

Nibbles Niblet was the king of transfiguration spells, but he was not known for using them on humans. It was rumored that he had once attempted changing a goat into a woman. As the story went, Nibbles had fallen in love with the goat, but he had gotten so embarrassed by what he had been doing that he channeled all his efforts to transmorph her into a human. And he had succeeded too. But after he married her, she became such a nag that he changed her back into a goat and rallied the town politicians to push for interspecies marriages.

Caterina Ogwern was another wizard that knew the craft well, and she had no qualms about using the spells on humans. She used those spells whenever the mood struck. But her mood swings cost her a guild status some fifty years ago and so she had moved to the Underworld.

The only wizard that Treneth knew who got involved in war transfigurations in the Upperworld was Peapod Pecklesworthy.

Treneth wondered at his former master. Why would he accept an undoing quest? There was too much difficulty keeping everyone in line, which would play against Whizzfiddle since he could barely keep himself in line.

In the morning, when Rimpertuz was feeling the effects of a night gone wrong, Treneth would get his information and Rimpertuz would get his just desserts.

A QUEST REMEMBERED

*A* loud thump brought Whizzfiddle out of his slumber. Morning always seemed to arrive much sooner than Whizzfiddle would have liked. It was followed by another thump.

He jumped from his bed and waited for his brain to join him. Grabbing his flask, he took a swig and felt his reserves begin to fill. Two more sips gave him enough energy to cast a spell that cleared his head and took the effects of his hangover away. One of these days he planned to bottle that spell so he could just drink the pain away.

His room came into focus and he peeked back at his bed to see if maybe he had a bed partner from the last evening. No such luck. The bedding was only ruffled on his side.

With a flick of his wrist, the knitted bedspread pulled itself back into place, revealing an embroidered red-and-yellow dragon smoking a cigar. The pillows were its eyes.

Another thump.

He drank the rest of the flask and crept toward the door, pausing only to grab his wand from the dresser. It was the one thing that, drunk or not, he managed to keep consistent every night. He didn't really need a wand to do magic. No wizard did. A lot of them went without them too, but Whizzfiddle felt that a wand added credibility to his profession.

As he slunk down the stairs there was a smell of cheese and roses. He thought this an odd combination and it certainly wasn't one he would subscribe to in his potpourri basket. The cheese, maybe, but never the roses.

There was a groan followed by a hush.

"You'll wake the wizard," a whispered voice said.

*Too late*, thought Whizzfiddle as he reached for his hat. His hat! He looked back toward his room and cursed himself. That pretty much sealed the fate of the intruders. Whizzfiddle was very private about his mood hair.

His magical resources were riding at about twenty percent. That didn't give him much to work with. Fortunately, his uninvited guests didn't know this.

With a final pounce, Whizzfiddle jumped around the corner with his wand at the ready.

"Ah-hah!"

There were four of them and they were all lying about in his living room.

"See?" a pimply elf said, not bothering to open his eyes. "I told you you'd wake him."

"What is the meaning of this?" Whizzfiddle demanded, wand whipping from head to head.

The scrawny knight stood up, raising his hands in surrender. He drifted behind the grandfather clock that sat next to the couch. "If you would kindly put the wand down, sir?"

"I think not," Whizzfiddle said. "Not until I understand your purpose, young man. However, I shall point it at your feet instead."

"Thank you, sir," the knight said, moving his feet out of

view. "After you accepted our quest we told you that we had no money to pay and you invited us to stay in your living room for the night."

Indeed, he had. An entire day of drinking at Gilly's can cause a person to forget all kinds of things. A little memory spell brought their names back to him. He hoped there was nothing else that he'd done that he couldn't recall.

"Sorry, lads," he said after a few moments of gathering himself, allowing his blood pressure to normalize. "It seems I was a little more blistered than I'd thought."

"You not remembering us?" Gungren said.

"Well, I do now," Whizzfiddle replied. "It's just when a wizard has a power base such as mine, the details get a little fuzzy until it all comes back."

"Sir?" Zel said, raising his hand.

"Yes?"

"Sorry. Um, well, your hair was bright red when you came in the room."

"Right, right," Whizzfiddle said. "It's a trick of the magic. I do that to put fear into the soul."

Orophin pushed himself up to one elbow. "Now it's kind of a yellowish color."

"Ah, yes, no point in keeping friends in fear, eh?"

"You teach me that?" Gungren asked.

"Pardon me," Bekner said.

"Uh oh."

"Not now, Bekner!"

"Not now what?" said Whizzfiddle.

The room rocked as the dwarf released his morning flatulence. Dwarfs were known for their uncanny volume, which could be heard echoing for miles in their underground labyrinths, but it would take a giant on a purely vegan diet to match the sonic boom of a seven-foot dwarf.

"You're a pig," Orophin said, waving his hands as Zel slid

back behind the grandfather clock and Whizzfiddle conjured up a large hand fan.

Bekner looked stunned. "What? I asked for a pardon."

"As if that makes it right," Orophin said.

The only one that didn't seem bothered was the little giant. Even Bekner's eyes were watering at his own scent.

"So, Mr. Wizard," Gungren asked again, "you teach me the hair trick?"

"Pardon me?" Whizzfiddle said.

"Oh no. Not you too."

"No, no," Whizzfiddle said. "I just meant I wanted clarification from our little friend here as to why he wanted to learn the magic trick."

"'Cause I are a wizard!"

"Is that so?"

"No," Orophin said. "He's not a wizard. He's a giant. Ever heard of a giant wizard?"

"Come to think of it, no."

"Of course you haven't," Orophin said. "There is no such thing. It was part of the change cast on him."

"Oh, that's right," said Whizzfiddle as more details filled in from his aging memory banks.

"I *are* a wizard," Gungren said.

"I *am* a wizard," Whizzfiddle corrected.

"Yeah," Gungren said, looking confused, "I know you is. So you teach me or not?"

"Or not," Whizzfiddle answered. "We are looking to have you all changed back, gentlemen. This means that you may not embrace your current state. The more you identify with who you've become the more challenging it will be to change you back."

"That the only reason I stay with them," Gungren harrumphed, pointing at the others. "I not need be here at all except for I want training."

46

The little giant sat with his arms and eyes crossed. Whizzfiddle was quite certain the arms were crossed on purpose.

"Sir," Zel interrupted cautiously, "your hair is kind of a greenish color now."

"Damn," Whizzfiddle said as he darted out of the room, hollering over his shoulder. "Let's get ready, gentlemen. We have much to do for our quest to start. And for the love of The Twelve, will somebody please open a window!"

## AN APPRENTICE PUNISHED

*T*reneth had finished his morning breakfast and strolled out to the garden.

The sun was out in force.

A cool breeze kept him comfortable as he took his seat under the golden raintree. His lilies were in full bloom, poking their white and red leaves over the neatly trimmed boxwoods. Treneth did so love his garden.

Rimpertuz was sprawled out on the grass and there were a number of ants crawling on him. Treneth reached his foot out far enough to give the man a kick in the buttocks.

Rimpertuz groaned.

"Morning has arrived, my apprentice. We have much to do today."

Rimpertuz rolled over and opened his eyes. He then slammed them shut and moaned again.

"I have no sympathy for you," Treneth said. "Get to your feet, man!"

It took a little time, but Rimpertuz managed to drag himself onto the adjacent bench. Grass littered Rimpertuz's matted hair, his shirt was ruffled and covered with stains that Treneth dare not wonder about, and his breath could be rivaled only by a latrine. It was unbecoming for an apprentice of Treneth of Dahl to look so disheveled.

"You are quite fortunate that I don't dismiss you outright and blight your name with the council."

"Yes, sir," Rimpertuz replied.

"It was an explicit part of our agreement that you would not partake in such dastardly conduct."

"Yes, sir."

"I have a mind to sever our agreement at this time, Rimpertuz."

"Yes, sir." Rimpertuz's eyes popped open. "Um...no, sir. Please, sir. It was a mistake, sir."

Treneth smiled to himself. His plans would have worked anyway, but now that his apprentice was in a groveling mood, things would go more smoothly.

He studied his hands for a moment, pretending to be deep in thought.

"Well," Treneth said, flicking a fly off his knee.

The fly was then more instantly drawn to Treneth's fingernails. With a small incantation, the fly's life ended in a puff of flame.

"Let it not be said that Treneth of Dahl is an unfair man."

"Certainly not, sir."

Rimpertuz need only say the magic words.

"I suppose if my apprentice were sufficiently sorry for his actions—"

"I am, sir."

"A man who does not feel great remorse over improper—"

"I do, sir. I truly do."

Treneth leaned back and slipped his gloves on. "I guess I could consider the circumstances."

"I'll do anything, sir," Rimpertuz said.

And there it was.

"Yes," Treneth replied. "You shall, Rimpertuz. And you will be thorough. I will not hear a negative word from you. And always be vigilant because I will be watching."

"Yes, sir. Vigilant, sir."

Treneth rose and headed back toward the kitchen. Rimpertuz was on his heel like a scolded puppy. They approached the house and Treneth put up a restraining hand, which Rimpertuz wisely shied away from.

"You're a mess, my apprentice. Here is what I require of you today, Rimpertuz. You will go and clean up, thoroughly. You will then run down to the guild and figure out some way to cause a diversion to make Whizzfiddle's attempt at getting a contract ratified difficult. When those two things are accomplished you may refill my magical supply and then clean up again. I will not see you until you have completed all of these things."

"Sir, I uh—"

"That will be all, Rimpertuz."

"It's just that, uh—"

Treneth tapped his foot.

"How would I delay Master Whizzfiddle, sir?"

"By using what little brains you have to be creative. I cannot provide you with every avenue for success, Rimpertuz. I will tell you that sometimes it helps to say a number of ideas aloud and one will just click with you."

Rimpertuz looked like a man whose light just came on. "Yes, sir. Again, sir, I do apologize."

"Yes, yes, I know." Treneth paused, trying to remember another point he'd had. "Ah, yes, did you ever see what was under the old man's hat?"

"No, sir. He kept it fastened the entire time. But I could continue following him, if—"

"You have other duties."

"Yes, but—"

"I would not wish to delay you further, my apprentice. Now," Treneth said as he began closing the door, "do move along."

# GUNGREN THE WIZARD?

*T*he group got a number of odd looks as they approached the town of Rangmoon, so Whizzfiddle decided to cut through the alleys instead. This is where all the houses that surrounded the city core were laid out.

Bekner had to duck under the clotheslines connected between the homes and everyone was careful to avoid patches of mud that had little chance of drying in the more shaded areas. Whizzfiddle had also warned Bekner to keep his sight straight ahead so as to avoid looking into bedroom windows.

A few people were out tilling their gardens. Whizzfiddle stopped occasionally to say his hellos while the others milled about.

When they broke out of the labyrinth of dwellings, Whizzfiddle was soured to see the line at the Wizards' Guild. It was unusually long for the middle of the week. It had been a good three years since Whizzfiddle had last registered a contract with the guild, though, so he assumed that times had gotten busier since Treneth had been pushing rules and regulations into all of the processes.

"This is going to take a while," he said and then blew out an exasperated breath.

"Maybe we should get something to eat first?"

"Aye," Bekner said. "Orophin's right. It takes loads of food to keep this new body fed."

Whizzfiddle didn't bother much with food these days. He had spent the last year working on lowering his daily intake because he had gotten a bit large. He was still rather round in the belly, due to drinking, and his bottom was admittedly wider than it should be, but overall he was half the size he was this time last year. Still, sometimes he got a bit famished, usually after drinking for a while, but that was rare. More often than not he'd get by with some bread and cheese and, of course, a bowl of stew.

"Bring me back some bread and cheese," Whizzfiddle said. "And don't dawdle, lads. If I get to the front and you're all gone I'll have to move to the back. Everyone has to sign the contract."

"Everyone?" Zel said.

"Is that a problem?"

"Um, no. I just—"

"It's fine," Orophin said, interrupting him. "Just make sure that the quill isn't too sharp or Zel may have problems holding it. Isn't that right, Zel?"

"Uh," Zel said, looking a bit unsure. The knight took a step back from Orophin, who was standing in the hand-on-hip, I-dare-you-to-disagree-with-me stance. "Yes," Zel squeaked. "That's right."

Whizzfiddle found the exchange a bit odd. Then he shrugged. Not much ordinary with this group.

"Wizards stay in line," Gungren piped up. "Hurry up. Us wizards got work to be done."

"It's 'we wizards,' Gungren," Whizzfiddle said as the others walked off toward town.

"That don't sound right."

"No," Whizzfiddle said, "I suppose it doesn't." He thought about it for a second and came to the conclusion that in the grand scheme of things, it didn't really matter. "Anyway," he said, "you're not a wizard, my little friend, and you need to keep such thoughts out of your head. It's only going to make this quest more difficult."

"But I are a wizard," Gungren insisted.

"Okay, I'll play. If you're a wizard, tell me what your power source is?"

"What?"

"Every wizard has a power source. Mine is alcohol, praise The Twelve, and yours is…?"

Gungren puffed out his chest and got a stern look on his face. "I not need none."

"Is that so? Well, then, let's see some magic, little wizard."

Gungren looked defiant for a few moments. He grabbed the leather pouch and rummaged through its contents, pulling it away as Whizzfiddle tried sneaking a peek inside. Mumbling to himself, he withdrew a stack of playing cards and set the pouch down. After a few moments of what could almost be called shuffling, he planted his feet and looked up at Whizzfiddle.

"Okay," Gungren said, "pick a card."

"Card tricks?"

"You want magic or no?"

Whizzfiddle took a deep breath. If Gungren did basic street magic, that wouldn't be as harmful as doing actual wizardly work. Still, even basic trickery and sleight of hand were tools in the most accomplished wizard's arsenal. It simply couldn't be encouraged.

"Fine," he said, and withdrew a card.

Gungren's face lit up. He really did seem to love magic, and that tugged at Whizzfiddle's heart. But it was only in Gungren's mind because of Pecklesworthy's spell. As soon as the spell was broken, Gungren would be back to his mindless enjoyment of throwing rocks.

Somehow this didn't make Whizzfiddle feel any better.

"Put card back in where my thumb are."

Whizzfiddle couldn't help but smile.

"As you say."

"Now," Gungrun said, pointing away, "you look that way for a second."

Whizzfiddle turned away and looked over at the line. It hadn't budged. Even yesterday when he had walked to town he hadn't noticed that the line was very long. Or, for that matter, the day before. Maybe Wednesdays, or Fridays, or whatever today was, had become the new day to get things done for wizards. They were creatures of habit, after all.

"Okay," Gungren said. "This your card?"

It wasn't his card. He'd had the three-of-boulders, but Gungren was holding up a six-of-pebbles. Everything to giants revolved around rocks of some sort. Whizzfiddle looked into Gungren's eyes and just couldn't deflate his hopes.

"My, my," he said, "it is indeed my card."

"Ha ha," Gungren said and bounced about. "No, it not!"

"Pardon?"

Gungren moved back.

"No, not that kind of pardon. I mean what do you mean that it's not my card?"

"You card was three-of-boulders." He held out the card. "See? But I showed six-of-pebbles."

"Ah, I must have forgotten, then."

"That 'cause Gungren put brain magic on you."

In a manner of speaking, Whizzfiddle thought, that is

exactly what happened. It was either hurt the little giant's feelings or make him think his magic wasn't working. Crush a dream or tell a white lie. But what if Gungren had made him feel this way? He shook his head. Not likely. Whizzfiddle chided himself for catering to the delusion in the first place.

"Okay, tiny man," Whizzfiddle said, "show me again."

"You know better," Gungren said, returning his cards to the pouch. "Wizards not show same trick twice."

## A BRIEF ALLIANCE

reneth slipped through the back of the guild, edging past the wooden filing cabinets while attempting to avoid wiping his freshly pressed shirt on the layer of dust covering everything. He made a mental note to have Rimpertuz give the place a fine cleaning once the plan for taking control of the council was complete. As a matter of point, he decided, everything in how the council and the guild was run would be cleaned up. It was an embarrassment.

Agnitine was sitting in her usual spot at the front desk.

Her station was meticulous: quills in their proper spot, or at least in the spot that Treneth, too, would have placed them, papers neatly arranged in stacks that were seemingly sorted by color, folders with labels attached just so, and not a speck of dirt, which was impressive considering how filthy the rest of the place was.

The only thing out of place was Agnitine herself.

Treneth did not like many people, including Agnitine, but she was one of the few he respected. She took her work seriously.

It was rare to see her lift her buttocks from her chair once the day began. It was difficult to watch her do so when the day ended, and one couldn't help but feel sorry for the chair. It was bent and rusted and looked to be compressed to a third of its original shape.

Agnitine was not one for healthy eating and daily exercise. Everyone had to have some flaw.

Treneth knew that Agnitine didn't see her excessive weight as a weakness. If anything, she relished it. On the weekends, she took to a new form of wrestling and was championed three times in as many years. Her fame only reinforced that she looked fine as she was, especially since she was never short of potential suitors.

The main lobby was deserted, which was not uncommon for this time of day. Treneth was hopeful that Rimpertuz had had something to do with it.

"Good morning, Agnitine," he said.

She peered over her shoulder and grunted. "Front door not good enough for you, Treneth?"

"How is business?"

"Booming," she said.

Treneth feigned a laugh. "I'm sure it's just slow at the moment."

Another grunt.

"It could be that the weather is holding everyone at home."

"Yeah, if people avoided sunny days."

"They're not for everyone."

"What do you want, Treneth?"

He shifted. "Are things well with your wrestling?"

"I'm still undefeated, as if you care," Agnitine said haughtily. "I think we both know that you didn't sneak in here to talk about the weather and my wrestling career."

"I'm injured, madam," he said as morosely as he could

fathom. "I feel that we have somewhere gotten off to a bad start."

"Maybe it was when you told Councilwoman Muppy that I was—how did you say it? Ah, yes—an 'overbearing *cow* of a woman.'"

Treneth cleared his throat. "Yes, well, I was clearly out of order. It had been a rough day, you see, and—"

"And when you publicly announced that 'livestock had no place working in the main office.'"

"Oh dear," said Treneth. "That comment had nothing to do with you."

"You were pointing directly at me when you said it."

"I'm sure I did not intend to."

"I'm sure you did." She sat back and crossed her arms. "What do you want, Treneth?"

"Oh fine." No point in exchanging pleasantries with this one. "I have a particularly annoying wizard who is determined to complete a quest, and I want to make sure that the contract he gets is worded so that he cannot slip through the cracks."

"*All* wizards are particularly annoying in one way or another. You are the only exception to that rule."

He blinked. "Oh?"

"You're *completely* annoying," Agnitine said with a smirk. "All the contracts are the same, Treneth, and you know it."

"This man is slippery, though."

"Name a wizard who isn't slippery," she said. "I see one noteworthy of the term in front of me right now."

"You know," Treneth said, clasping his hands behind his back, "one day I will be in charge of the council. When that day arrives, some people will still be working and some people will not be."

"I make more money wrestling than I do here anyway."

"Ah yes, but how many more years will you be able to

wrestle? And what, The Twelve forbid, will you do if some tragic accident were to befall you?"

With a motion far too swift for a woman of her size, Agnitine was on her feet, the chair flying in the opposite direction.

"Is that a threat?" Her stare was icy. "Please tell me that was a threat."

"Of course not," he said hoarsely. "I wouldn't even imagine such a thing. I merely meant in the grand scheme of things, you know?"

He squirmed around her and snatched up the chair, sliding it back in position for her.

"Wrestling is a dangerous sport."

She thundered back down into the chair, dropping to within inches of the floor. It took a few moments for it to rise back to its original height and Treneth could have sworn it made a crying sound.

"Not the way I wrestle," Agnitine said.

"Fair enough," he said. "Yet there is still the possibility."

"I've got savings."

"I'm sure you do."

"Look, little man, I don't have all day to sit here and talk to you about my job. Now, what are you trying to accomplish with this contract?"

"It's nothing, really."

"Spit it out, Treneth."

"Yes, well," he said and cleared his throat, "I would like to put in some direct wording."

"You know that's against regulations."

It figured that the one thing he admired about Agnitine was the one thing that would get in his way. He would do the same thing if he were in her shoes. Not that he could fit in her shoes. Nor would he try. Treneth was not that type of guy.

"Yes, but sometimes regulations are not sturdy enough."

She tilted her head slightly. "I'm listening."

"Agnitine, you and I do not see eye-to-eye on a number of things."

"I can't name one."

"Ah," he said, grinning, "but there is one. We are both sticklers for doing what needs to be done, and right now there is a man on his way here who is looking to get a contract to fulfill a sentence bestowed upon him by the guild council."

"Whizzfiddle."

"Indeed."

"He's never missed one of my events, you know."

"Is that so?" Treneth said as his heart sank.

"Yes, that's so," she replied.

Treneth's brain was pouring out expletives that his mouth would never utter. That was one of many problems in getting even with Whizzfiddle. He knew everyone, and everyone liked him. Easy to get along with. Always willing to buy someone an ale and have a long chat about nothing. Loved music and puppies. Good old Whizzfiddle. Blech!

"The bastard always bets against me," Agnitine said finally.

"Is that so?" Treneth repeated, feeling more amazed than defeated.

"If he catches the change in the contract, he'll have every right to request a new one, and it'll be my ass if he decides to complain."

"As to that," Treneth said, "let's just say that Master Whizzfiddle is not one for looking at details. He's cunning, yes; scrupulous, no."

She drummed her fingers on the desk.

"Fine," she said, "but you owe me one, Treneth."

"Certainly, certainly."

"My next match," she said, cracking her knuckles. "You'll be there and you'll put a nice bet on me to win."

"Me? A wrestling match?"

"Make sure you wear one of those fine suits, too." Agnitine looked him over. It was a hungry look. It was not a look Treneth was used to having bestowed upon him. "I like my audience to inspire my lust for contact."

He swallowed hard.

"Understand?" she added with a wink.

Treneth felt the blood drain from his face as he quivered a nod.

Agnitine burst into laughter.

"I'm joking, Treneth! You actually quite disgust me, and I don't want you lowering the class of my matches. But it was quite worth it to watch you squirm."

She handed him the contract as he struggled to decide whether to feel relieved, irritated, or both.

"Make the changes and I'll make sure Whizzfiddle gets it when he comes in."

# THE LINE

*I* don't understand what's taking so long," Whizzfiddle said. "I've never seen a line like this at the guild."

He leaned out a bit but couldn't see around the litany of people. He tried jumping, but he wasn't that tall and his portly stature gave gravity the edge. It was also irritating that Gungren mimicked his every move.

"Gungren, keep our spot like a good lad. I'm going to go see what's happening."

Whizzfiddle moved up, looking from person to person along the way and saying his hellos, when he suddenly realized that none of them were wizards.

He stopped when he saw one of the local farmers.

"Idoon?"

"Master Whizzfiddle," Idoon said, putting out his hand for a shake. "Good to see you, sir. I've got a fresh batch of apples waiting for you at the farm. I know you like the dark red ones."

"Lovely, and I thank you."

"It's no problem at all. I can deliver them to your porch, if you'd like, sir."

"That would be splendid, yes, although I will be out of town for a while. A wizardly quest, you see." He pointed to his backpack. "It may be better if you can get them to Gilly's in the next hour or so. Yes, that would be ideal."

Whizzfiddle slipped the man a gold piece, which was ransom for only twenty batches of apples, but the elderly wizard had more than enough money to go around.

"Thank you, sir! Always a pleasure providing the finest fruits and vegetables to you, sir."

"If you don't mind my asking, Idoon," Whizzfiddle said, "why are you in line?"

"Oh, well, that young man Rimpertuz handed me a silver piece a short while ago and said I could keep it if I just stood here for a while."

"Is that right?"

"Yes, sir," Idoon said, scratching his ear. "Seemed a bit odd to me, sir, but a silver goes a long way these days."

"I imagine it does, yes," Whizzfiddle said kindly. "If you'll excuse me?"

"Certainly, sir. Thank you again, sir."

Whizzfiddle smiled, reached up, and patted Idoon on the shoulder before he moved farther up the line. He spotted Heathnip Clippersmith, the local barber, Saldinia, the stable master, and various other people who had little reason to engage in guild business.

He sighed and laughed to himself. Treneth was a clever one.

"Excuse me, ladies and gentleman…"—he spotted Barben Tallendure, the tailor, who was also an elf—"…and, uh, Barben." Barben scowled as the others in line snickered. "Is anyone here on guild business?"

All the heads wiggled a definitive no, except for one rather bulbous one near the back of the line.

"Yes, Gungren," Whizzfiddle shouted, waving. "I know why you're here."

A few moments later, Whizzfiddle walked through the main door of the guild building with Gungren in tow. He was hot and miffed, but every wizard knew better than to approach Agnitine when in a foul mood, for her foul mood was most foul indeed.

"Gungren," he said, "wait for the others and then bring them through those double doors. We'll not be able to complete the contract without them, but I can get the groundwork in place."

"Yes, master."

Whizzfiddle took a step toward the door and stopped. "What was that?"

"What were what?"

"Know this, little giant, I am *not* your master. I no longer accept apprentices and you are *not* a wizard." Gungren reached for his cards. "Card tricks aside, without a proper power source, you are merely a street magician." Whizzfiddle squatted down. "I know it's hard to hear this, Gungren, but there is no sense in believing a lie."

Gungren sighed, looking downcast.

"Yes, master."

"There, that's better... Wait, no."

He grabbed Gungren by the shoulders and stared directly into his eyes.

"Again, I am *not* your master," he said, saying each word distinctly. "Understand?"

"Yes, master."

"Good," Whizzfiddle said, and walked through the double doors.

CONTRACTS

gnitine smiled at Whizzfiddle when he approached the counter. That was irregular. Treneth was standing back by one of the filing cabinets, working on a document. Agnitine smiling while Treneth was within proximity was downright deviant.

"Long line out there today," Whizzfiddle said in Treneth's general direction.

"Is that so?"

"Good morning, Agnitine."

"So far," she said.

He would need to keep his guard up.

"I'm in need of a contract. There will be multiple signatures and a fixed timeline."

"One month," Treneth piped up and then slid the document over to Agnitine. "I have already put in the dates for you, my friend."

Whizzfiddle snorted. Friend? Hardly. He'd just as soon befriend a vampire. It pained him, too, that he thought such a thing since he tried to treat everyone—including vampires—

equally. It was just something people said in the Upperworld. He sighed.

"Anxious to see me succeed, eh, Treneth?"

"I can think of nothing I want more."

"I'm sure. Let me see this contract so I can fill in the quest details."

"I am somewhat impressed with you, truth be told. A Quest of Undoing is a difficult one."

Whizzfiddle didn't bother looking up from his writing. "I wonder how, pray tell, that you knew it was a Quest of Undoing?"

"I, uh," Treneth continued, "saw a very large dwarf walking down the street with you today, and I just made the connection."

"I'm sure," Whizzfiddle murmured.

The paperwork took some time to fill out. Fifteen minutes later, the troop arrived. Bekner had to stoop a bit to get through the door and Orophin had various sauces on his shirt. It was appalling to see an elf in such disarray.

"It's about time," Whizzfiddle said. "We haven't the luxury to... What's that word? I said it earlier."

"Dawdle," Zel said.

"Yes, that's it." Whizzfiddle wasn't used to this work-ethic mentality. "We have...uh-hem...work to do."

Agnitine reached up and snatched the contract from Whizzfiddle. She looked it over and pointed at each person in the party, counting them.

"It looks like everyone is present," she said. "Okay, Whizzfiddle, you sign first and then whatever order the rest of you signs doesn't matter."

The last to sign was Gungren, but he began reading through the document. Whizzfiddle had expected the little giant would just put an inkblot on the page since giants didn't know how to write. Evidently, they knew how to read.

"Are you actually reading that or just looking at the symbols?"

"Shh," Gungren held up the same finger Whizzfiddle did to convey pause. "I are busy."

Pecklesworthy must have really put some power into this transfiguration. Not only was Gungren deluding himself into believing that he, a giant, could be a wizard, the runt could read!

"Nope," Gungren said after a few minutes, "I not signing this."

"What?"

"I not signing this," he repeated. "It need fixed first."

"Listen, Gungren," Whizzfiddle said, "I'm beginning to lose my patience with you, and anyone who knows me will tell you that's a difficult task."

"Master," Gungren whispered, pointing at the document, "you not read this. It say here that you got only got thirty hours to finish, not thirty days."

"What?" Whizzfiddle took the document and studied it.

*"The wizard will have a full thirty days to complete this quest, and must do so to the letter of the contract. A day, as modified and accepted through the signing of this contract, equates exactly to a single turn of the clock."*

"I don't see the problem," Whizzfiddle said.

"Single turn of clock."

"Right."

"That an hour, not a day."

Whizzfiddle glowered at Treneth, who appeared busily working on another contract. Treneth was a by-the-book wizard, but the book he followed was written from his own hand.

Whizzfiddle wrote "VOID" on the contract and then ripped it in two.

"Well done, Gungren," said Whizzfiddle. "Agnitine, I shall

require a new contract. This time, I shall take one from the middle of the stack, if you please."

PROVISIONS

*R*angmoon was a town in motion.

There were carts, buggies, and pedestrians all about. Street performers jostled for prime locations in the center square. Beggars held to the alleys, mostly, venturing out cautiously now and again for a quick request and then disappearing back into the shadows before being spotted by a footman.

The shops were doing well these days. Rangmoon's economy always picked up in the spring. People just seemed happier and that led to spending money on new outfits, polished saddles, and candied treats. While this was good for Rangmoon, it was trying on Whizzfiddle's schedule.

The elderly wizard looked at the position of the sun for a moment, calculating.

"Gentlemen," he said, "it is precisely early afternoon or so. I wish to be out of this city and on our way by late afternoon. We have much to do and little time to do it."

"But we've got—"

"Thirty days. Yes, I know, Beckner. However, these types of quests have the potential for simplicity or complexity." He began checking each pocket to find his coin purse. "I have been known to attract the latter type of situations, so I don't want to take any chances. A quick start and finish will be a wise course of action."

Whizzfiddle pulled out a handful of change. "I am giving each of you three gold pieces. That should be more than enough for any supplies you may deem necessary to bring along on this journey. Most of these supplies will be emergency use only, but don't neglect the fact that on any quests there are always emergencies. Yes, Zel?"

Zel put his hand down.

"Are we to bring food and drink?"

"You were a knight, were you not?"

"Well, yes."

"And you never had to prepare for going out on a quest?"

"Certainly, yes, but we had people to prepare—"

"I'll take care of it," Orophin said. "Just come along with me."

Whizzfiddle took a sip from his flask as he headed off toward Gilly's.

He set on casting tiny spells that transferred small bits of change from his purse into the pockets of the beggars. Most of them were either friends or relatives of long-dead friends, and he never did much like seeing the young ones in such a state.

A thought struck him.

"Beggars," he hollered. "Come speak with me, if you would."

He had a small crowd within moments. A couple of footmen stepped over as well.

"I will be leaving for a quest this very afternoon," Whizzfiddle said. "This means that I will have need for the grounds of my property to be taken care of as well as protected. Most of you know where I live?" There were nods all around. "This will not be easy work, mind. The grass can get unwieldy and the garden needs a critical eye."

The grass was already out of control and the garden was dead because Whizzfiddle had little inclination to do work nor did he have a critical gardening eye.

"Who is interested in taking up this task?"

All hands went up, including one of the footmen. The other footman pushed his partner's arm back down.

"Well and good," Whizzfiddle said. "The pay will be a one gold per week."

Both of the footmen put their hands up.

"You will be able to stay in the shed next to the house."

"All of us?" Sander, an old friend of Whizzfiddle's, asked.

"Correct. Don't let it fool you, there is a lot of room in that shed." The shed had a nice magical field placed upon it that widened its innards quite a bit. The only rub was that if Whizzfiddle was away for more than a year, the shed would slowly return to its normal shape. "Sander, I will need someone to be in charge of this. As I recall, you ran your own business for some time, no?"

"Yessir, I ran the rent-a-casket business, sir."

"Ah, yes," Whizzfiddle recalled thoughtfully. "It did seem a good idea at the time."

"On paper, sir. As you had said, sir."

It was a good idea, on paper. The problem was that the pay-as-you-go plan was too frequently replaced with you-went-before-you-paid. Plus, families weren't too keen on their loved one's caskets being repossessed, and Sander didn't have the sinisterness to exact such measures anyway.

"I believe you're the man for the job," Whizzfiddle said and then flung a spell at him. A little grouping of sparkles surrounded Sander's head and then dissipated. "You'll have access to my house, but nobody else will be able to go in.

Anyone who tries will get a nice jolt at the door. Please do be mindful of that as I've heard that it rather stings."

Their faces were all pale. Sander beamed.

"One last thing," Whizzfiddle said, motioning everyone to follow him to Kope's Bathhouse, "I want you all cleaned up and kept cleaned up."

Kope had an expression of horror as Whizzfiddle approached.

"Kope," Whizzfiddle said, bowing slightly.

"Master Whizzfiddle, sir."

Whizzfiddle pulled out a number of gold coins. He began piling them into Kope's hands. The Bathhouse usually charged a single silver for a thorough cleaning. Whizzfiddle provided enough funds to clean his new "employees" for a year.

"Six months of cleanings for all you see here," Whizzfiddle said to a stunned Kope.

"Yes, sir. Thank you, sir."

"Excuse me?" One of the footmen had stepped up, helmet tucked respectfully under his arm. "Does that include us, sir?" The man was shuffling a bit. "It's been a while since...um...my partner here had a nice cleaning."

"What?" his partner said.

"I suppose the house could use some protection against thieves," Whizzfiddle said, smiling inwardly. "Three passes a day, including weekends. Are we in agreement?"

They both saluted, if it could be called that.

"Very well." Whizzfiddle added a few more coins to Kope's stash.

## CALLING IN A FAVOR

*R*impertuz," Treneth said as his apprentice was shoveling ostrich feces into a barrel, "I have immediate need of assistance."

Rimpertuz laid the shovel down and approached. When he got within a few feet of Treneth, there was a change of plan.

"Actually, it can wait," Treneth said, waving away the stench. "First you'll need to wash up and *then* I'll need immediate assistance."

"Yes, sir."

"Hurry to it, man. Time is of the essence."

Rimpertuz trotted off toward his humble lodgings.

Treneth entered his office, creaking the floorboard and cringing slightly. *Vigilance*, he thought.

He sat and pulled open the lower drawer and sighed. He hated to do it, but the contract sabotage had failed. With a groan, he pulled forth a device that looked like a hammer with two heads. One head was placed on the ear and the other was sidled to the mouth. In its center sat a grouping of buttons that were etched with numbers and letters. It was an

Underworld device that he had only used once, and that was just to test it. It was named the "TalkyThingy."

Treneth snagged a piece of paper from the drawer and plunked in the numbers and then pressed the red button. After a moment, a buzzing sound emitted from one of the hammer-heads.

"Yeah," a voice said.

"Yes, hello?"

"Yeah," the voice repeated.

"Uh," Treneth said as he felt sweat beading on his forehead, "I would like to speak to Teggins, please."

"You got him."

"I've got him?"

"This *is* Teggins," he said.

"Oh, I see. This is Master Treneth of Dahl."

"Well, well, well," Teggins said at length. "It's been five years or better, Treneth of Dahl."

"Yes," Treneth said, slumping his shoulders and then jumping straight back to attention. One had to remain in control. "Can you see me?"

"No, Treneth," Teggins said, "but I could hear you slumping."

"You could?"

"No," Teggins laughed. "It was a guess. So what do I owe the pleasure of the great wizard calling into the Underworld?"

The damnable technology always set Treneth on edge. He saw no point whatsoever in replacing the natural flowing of magical energies with manmade contraptions that, at best, made people lazier than they already were. He had to agree that the mechanical zappers did do well for keeping vampires away, but that was an anomaly.

When Teggins had originally given the TalkyThingy to Treneth, he had explained that it worked by sending some type of wave through the air to the nearest portal, which then tracked it to the portal hub and through a series of switches and whatnots until it connected to the appropriate party on the other side. Most of the description made little sense to Treneth. There were too many words and acronyms that sat outside of his vocabulary and there weren't many books in the Upperworld that could supply definitions for even a tenth of them. The mere thought of one's voice traveling such grand distances faster than a wizard could transport a letter, and with far less power expenditure, was just unsettling.

Treneth abhorred the fact that he had resorted to fraternizing with the Underworlder in the first place. But he had to cover all of his bases when working against one such as Whizzfiddle and when planning his own usurpation of the council. So Treneth closed his eyes and said the unthinkable.

"I...need a favor."

"Do you now?" Teggins said. "Last I recall, I'd asked you for a favor and you got back to me five years later asking me for a favor instead."

"You...what?"

"You were supposed to clear my name with the guild, Treneth."

Treneth was now in his element. Negotiation.

"Yes, Teggins, I was and I am. As you may also recall, I had said, clearly and repeatedly, that it would take me upwards of twenty years to get to such a level where I could assist."

"Okay, okay," Teggins said. "Don't turn your britches into butt-floss."

Treneth mulled that over for a moment and gave up.

"I am nearly on the council as we speak," Treneth continued. "I would imagine I will be able to assist you in your plight within the next month, even."

"Is that so?"

"Yes, that is so," Treneth replied. "First, though, I shall need some assistance from you."

"I'll bite. What?"

"There is a man coming into the Underworld on a Quest of Undoing."

"Which one is that?" Teggins said.

"The man?"

"No, the Quest of Undoing. What is that?"

Treneth remembered that the Underworlders were mostly magically devoid, but they were quick learners. Even with many wizards from the Upperworld moving down to garner freedom from guild rules and regulations, the locals weren't all that fond of magic and so they kept their distance. Essentially, they felt about magic as Treneth felt about technology. It kept the balance. Teggins was different, though. As soon as this call was over, he would likely assign one of his minions to gather details on every facet of the quest type.

"It's a simple quest where people are changed physically and mentally. Then a wizard is hired to get them back to what they were."

"Oh, like turning one of them prince-types into a frog kind of thing?"

"Close enough," Treneth said.

"So what do you need from me?" Teggins asked.

"I need you to delay him."

"Okay, so who is it?"

"Whizzfiddle."

"Xebdigon?"

"Unless you know of another Whizzfiddle."

"How do you want him delayed?"

"However you see fit."

"Well, I'm not going to kill him. He's a friend of my old mother."

"Of course not," Treneth said. "I'm sure you can find ways of applying delays as I continue working on getting your release to return to the Upperworld."

"I'll do my part, Treneth. Just make sure you do yours."

After they hung up, Treneth took a few moments to compose himself. Working with technology made him feel dirty. It was like using magic without the essence, which, in Treneth's case, made technology a cleaner option.

# THE CONFESSION

The lunch rush was over by the time Whizzfiddle got to Gilly's pub. Since Gilly's was not known for its food, the lunch rush consisted of a flock of no-goods drinking off their hangovers.

"Gilly?" he called out as he approached the bar.

Gilly was wiping his hands on a dirty rag as he came out from the kitchen.

"Good day, Master Whizzfiddle," Gilly said. "Already have your supplies ready."

"You do?"

"Well, you were in for a quest yesterday, sir," Gilly said with a wink.

"Indeed," Whizzfiddle said. "Good man, Gilly. How many have you got for me?"

"Seven, sir, but I can do more if needed."

Seven mini-barrels over thirty days. It should suffice, but he would have preferred ten to be on the safe side. Not for the magical potency, but rather because he liked Gilly's ale.

"Seven should do," he said. "If you're able to place one more together quickly, though, I would not complain."

Gilly called out to have his sons head into the cellars for another barrel as Whizzfiddle doled out triple the going rate. The elderly wizard knew it was wise to keep all his contacts happy, and to keep his ale supplier ecstatic.

Whizzfiddle grabbed his backpack and placed it on the ground near the casks. He opened its mouth wide and grabbed for the frothy mug that Gilly had laid out for him. With each pull from the mug, he said a little incantation that brought one of the drums smoothly over and into the backpack. As soon as it touched the brim, it shrank to the size of a mug and slipped neatly inside. Gilly's sons arrived with the last one, giving Whizzfiddle a little buffer.

"Did Idoon bring my apples?"

Gilly pointed to the table next to the door where sat an oversize bushel of dark reds. A flick of the wrist sent those hiding into the pack as well. A few purchases of dried meat and blocks of cheese, and Whizzfiddle said his goodbyes and trucked out the door.

The rest of the troop were ready to go as well.

"I see that one of you didn't listen very well," Whizzfiddle said, looking at Gungren, who sported a new purple-colored wizardly hat with little designs on it.

"I told him it was a nay thing to be after purchasing," Bekner said.

"And you were right to do so. Yes, Zel?"

"Sorry, sir," Zel said. "I brought foodstuffs and drink only, sir. Is that all well?"

Whizzfiddle frowned. "Would that be what you would bring on a knight's journey?"

"Yes, sir."

"Then, *Knight* Zelbaldian Riddenhaur—"

"Former knight, sir."

"—I would say that you are well-suited for our trip. And please do stop raising your hand when you have a question."

"Yes, sir."

"How are we going to be completing this quest if Gungren keeps after wizarding?" Bekner asked, plucking Gungren's hat.

"It becomes more and more challenging, actually. It would behoove you all to keep a critical eye on each other."

He scanned each of them. The problem child was obviously Gungren, but Zel's cowardice didn't help. Orophin was clearly unhappy with his looks, and not many dwarfs would find pleasure in being as large as Bekner.

Whizzfiddle led them out of the city. They were making good time and Whizzfiddle toyed with the idea of taking an afternoon nap. The thought tugged at him as they passed his house but he pushed steadfast toward a clearing in the surrounding forest.

Zel was whispering something back and forth with Orophin during the entire walk. Whizzfiddle couldn't make out what it was. No matter. It was obvious that Zel was the target of Orophin's interest, even if the elf denied it. There was simply too much flirting going on from Orophin's side.

Bekner stayed close to Gungren.

"Ye gonna be after ruining it for us all, Gungren."

"No, I not."

"Ye shall and ye know it."

"You not know nothing. I be a great wizard and then you have nothing to say."

"That's the point," Bekner admonished. "Ye should be after being a giant, not a great wizard."

Whizzfiddle was pleased to hear the seed had been planted. Working through the details of a quest posed enough complexity. He could use a little help from the rest of the troop to keep each other in line. After all, this wasn't a babysitting quest...yet.

For now, he had to worry about getting from point A to

point B as smoothly as possible, and that meant they had to find the portal. This was always a tricky task because grass and foliage grew at a higher rate around the portal area. One of his troll friends had explained that this was due to the type of energy that emanated from the device.

"It would be easier if we knew what we were looking for," said Orophin.

"Aye," agreed Bekner as he hurdled a large log deep into the woods.

Whizzfiddle itched at his nose, thinking. "It's a flat, square rock about the size of a small table," he said absently as he kicked away dirt and branches. "It will be flush with the ground."

"This it?" Gungren said, pointing at a small marble sphere that hovered a foot off the ground.

"Not according to the wizard's description," Orophin said.

Whizzfiddle stepped up to the orb and placed his hands on either side. He whispered a cryptic passcode, "takemebelow," and then stepped back. The ball flashed for a moment and then disappeared, leaving a square in the ground that was about the size of a table. A small metallic arm stuck out of its farthest edge.

"What is it?" Orophin said.

"It's called a portal," Whizzfiddle replied. "We are going to be going to a number of places that will seem strange to you. There will be dangers and... Yes, Zel?"

"There is another," Zel said quickly.

"Zel!" Orophin snapped, causing Zel to run behind Bekner.

"I'm sorry," Zel said meekly, "but I can't stand the deception any longer!"

"Pardon me?" Whizzfiddle said. They all stepped back. He

sighed. "Would someone mind telling me what Zel is talking about?"

The former knight was shaking as Orophin glared at him. Finally, the elf threw up his hands, sat down on a nearby rock, and motioned Zel to go ahead.

"There was another one in our group when we were transformed."

"What?" Whizzfiddle shouted, feeling his blood begin to steam.

It was going to be difficult enough saving his guild status in this quest and now this? Why was it that every quest he went on was full of surprises? Couldn't there just be one or two that went smoothly? Was that truly too much to ask for?

"Don't blame him," Orophin said. "It was my idea to keep it from you."

"May I ask why you felt the need to do such a thing?" Whizzfiddle said.

"Because we tried a number of wizards and they all turned us down. You gave us a 'yes' and we didn't want you to back out."

Whizzfiddle kicked a few rocks and threw others. Gungren began doing the same thing.

"Stop that," Whizzfiddle said, wagging a finger at Gungren. "You are not a wizard. Quit trying to be one."

"I are too," Gungren said, hands on his hips.

"Anything else you're not telling me?" Whizzfiddle asked Orophin.

"No."

"Where is he...or is it a she?"

"Kind of an it, really," Bekner said. "He's a lizard."

"A lizard."

"He *was* a dragon," Zel said, "but he was changed into, yes, a lizard."

Whizzfiddle knew a number of dragons.

"What is this dragon's name?"

"Winchester," Orophin said.

"Winchester Hargrath?"

"Yes, sir," Zel replied.

"Okay, here is the important part: Is it Winchester Hargrath Junior, or"—he swallowed hard—"Winchester Hargrath Junior the Third?"

"The third, I believe," Orophin said.

"That's right, yes," Zel affirmed.

*Wonderful*, thought Whizzfiddle. Junior wasn't so bad. He wasn't very bright. Junior, III, though, was one of the more astute dragons. Winchester always had an angle and a plan, and anything else he could fit up his sleeve. Whizzfiddle spat. Bringing Winchester would prove troublesome.

"It no matter anyway," Gungren said. "Him not sign contract so you not need him for quest."

"Were it that easy, I would be elated," Whizzfiddle replied. "A Quest of Undoing ties you all together. It *can* be undone without all of you, yes, but it's much more difficult."

"Why?"

"Because it's a group spell. It's like trying to complete a puzzle that doesn't have all the pieces. Do we have any idea where Winchester is?"

"Not exactly," Zel said. "He said something about starting up a business where there would be likenesses on paper of scantily-clad women."

"Pictures?" Whizzfiddle said. "Scantily-clad women?" He looked around for a moment and then snapped his fingers. "Dakmenhem. He's in Dakmenhem."

"I ain't rightly heard of that place," Beckner said.

"Nor would you have. It's in the Underworld."

## THE SHIPMENT

*T*reneth was sitting at his desk when Rimpertuz arrived, freshly scrubbed from his day's toil. While there were many negatives to having an apprentice with the paltry cognitive capabilities of Rimpertuz, there were advantages to it as well. It had been years since Treneth had lifted a shovel, for example.

"Rimpertuz," he said, "I feel it may be time for you to begin planning your future. You need to do things you can really own, you see?"

"I do?"

"Would I say so if it weren't true?"

Rimpertuz didn't reply.

"Your ingenuity with delaying Whizzfiddle at the guild was impressive, to say the least."

"It was?"

"Absolutely. I dare say that I was proud of you."

"You were?"

"That said, I feel it is time for you to build relationships with other wizards. This will be done of your own volition."

"Um—"

"There is a wizard who lives in Kek," Treneth said. "His name is Peapod Pecklesworthy. It seems that his birthday is coming up."

"Yes, sir. His birthday."

"As an apprentice begins to grow, it is often wise to glean support in the eyes of those who may one day be of assistance to him."

"But you always said that other wizards are stupid and foolish, and you always have falling outs with—"

"I am not your average wizard, Rimpertuz," Treneth said sternly. "I am self-reliant. You, on the other hand, are not."

"No, sir," Rimpertuz responded without looking offended.

If there was any one thing that Treneth held as confidence regarding Rimpertuz it was that Rimpertuz had little in the way of confidence.

"What, then," questioned Treneth, "would you say could be a wise move to garner some favor from Master Pecklesworthy?"

Rimpertuz pursed his lips. He began pacing and mumbling as well, stepping repeatedly on the loose floorboard in the process. Treneth allowed this to continue for a while before deciding to offer some assistance.

"It *is* the man's birthday."

"A gift!"

"A gift, you say? Hmmm, that's rather ingenious, my apprentice."

"It is? Yes, I mean…yes, that's right. Ingenious."

"What kind of gift, though?" Treneth tapped his desk. "I wouldn't want to influence your decisions here."

"It's okay, sir. What should I get him?"

"No, really, I don't want to get involved with your quest.

Unless, of course, you are asking me because it is part of your quest? That would be a different matter entirely."

Rimpertuz pulled out a little notebook and began fishing around for a writing instrument. Treneth withheld a sigh, opened his desk drawer, and grabbed one of his own. He handed it to his apprentice.

"Sir," Rimpertuz said formally, "I am, um, doing a quest on my own."

"Is that so?"

"Yes, sir. That's okay, right? I mean you were saying that I should—"

"It's fine, Rimpertuz," Treneth responded, almost feeling sad for how dimwitted the man could be. "I'm just happy to see you taking some initiative."

"Thank you, sir." Rimpertuz was beaming. "Um, I was wondering if you knew what a good gift may be for Master Pinkelhurley?"

"It's Pecklesworthy," Treneth said, spelling it out as Rimpertuz wrote. "I suppose a box of cigars would be nice. Hmmm, no, I don't believe he smokes cigars." Treneth crossed his fingers and looked off in mock-thought. "A new pair of slippers is always a useful gift, but that could come across as a bit too personal." Treneth continued the play as Rimpertuz was writing and then scratching out idea after idea. Once Rimpertuz had gotten to page three, Treneth felt it was time to drop a solid hint. "I guess the obvious one would be his magical source. Every wizard is in constant need of that store."

A moment or two passed.

"Do you happen to know Master Pickleherpie's magic source, sir? That may be a good gift, yes?"

"It's Pecklesworthy, and *that* is an inspired idea, Rimpertuz."

Rimpertuz puffed out his chest. "I once heard that every wizard is in constant need of their magical store, sir."

"Just recently, no doubt," Treneth said under his breath. "Yes, well, un-shucked pea pods are his source, my apprentice."

"Pea pods?"

"*Un-shucked* pea pods, to be exact."

"Any idea where I could get those?"

"Farmer Idoon, Rimpertuz," Treneth said with an amazed groan.

"I just saw him earlier today, sir. I'll ask him to ship a box of pea pods up to Kek straightaway, then."

"Just remember that a late present is not as promising as an early one, and do underline the fact that they must be *un-shucked* pea pods."

"I'll expedite the shipping."

"Let me give you a word of advice," Treneth said, trying to drive the point home and make sure that things ended the way he wanted them to. "Tell Idoon that you will pay double his costs if the shipment leaves by tomorrow morning, and that you will provide an additional twenty-five-percent bonus if they arrive on time. Fifty percent if early."

"That's a great idea, sir!"

"I do try," Treneth replied. "Also, you may consider sending a healthy supply indeed. What better gift than, say, a year's helping of one's power source? That would make quite an impression indeed, no?"

Rimpertuz looked excited before he frowned.

"Sir," he said as he shuffled his feet, "I don't really make much money as an apprentice."

"Ah, yes." Treneth grabbed his coin purse. "I would happily *loan* you enough to cover ten—"

"Twenty!"

Treneth raised his eyebrows at Rimpertuz.

"I want to do this right, sir."

As an excited Rimpertuz scuttled purposefully out the door with ample coin in hand, Treneth smiled and rapped his desk.

"Sometimes it really is too easy," he said to the empty room.

## LIZARDS AND LOAN SHARKS

*W*inchester Hargrath Jr. III was still getting used to seeing the world from his new size. Spending thousands of years as a creature that could extend its height upwards of thirty feet made for a rather large juxtaposition to now only being able to rise a few inches.

In fact, Winchester had decided that being little had afforded him the ability to explore life in an entirely new way.

As a dragon, he'd spent most of his days sleeping in a pile of gold, and he was always being hunted. The only chance he got to be clever was when he was dropping riddles on would-be thieves before devouring them, or if he was hired to defend an army. He would never have been able to walk around Dakmenhem, talk to the locals, or start up his own business in the town.

While it was quite a change in how he viewed the world, Winchester found the entire ordeal fascinating. The thought of being a dragon again wasn't even appealing. If anything it was bothersome; he was getting used to being so tiny. He was acclimating as best he could, but this hanging upside stuff was nauseating.

"So where the dough?" said Curdles, the local crime boss. He was holding Winchester precariously over a grinder by the tail.

If Winchester could sweat, he would have.

"I just need a little more time," Winchester said.

"Oh," Curdles said to Zooks and Yultza, a couple of henchpeople, "he needs a little more time."

Zooks chuckled in that not-so-funny way. Yultza wasn't the laughing type. Winchester found her to be dreadfully serious, which he decided was immensely attractive. Of all the orcs Winchester had met in his lifetime, Yultza was by far the most horrendous…in a good way.

"You could just drop me and be out of a hundred gold completely."

Curdles scowled. The mob boss didn't like to be reasoned with. Not many orcs did.

"Your dragon tricks aren't going to work on me, lizard."

Winchester crossed his arms, adopting as stoic a visage as he could manage.

"It's not a trick, Curdles. It's simple logic. If you drop me, how will you regain your hundred gold?"

"Seems I won't regain it whether I drop you or not."

"Now, that's unfair," Winchester said. "You lent me ten gold upon my arrival and I paid you back fifteen within two weeks."

"Yeah, out of the hundred that I lent you the second time."

"Well, yes, that's true, but I could have simply stepped away with the full one hundred and been in your debt one hundred and ten now."

Curdles looked thoughtful for a moment and then clicked off the grinder and pushed it out of the way. He dropped Winchester on the desk.

"I don't know why," Curdles said, "but I like you, Winchester."

"I am quite likable."

"Nope, that ain't it. I think it's because I like the thought of having my own pet dragon."

"Pet?"

"Yeah," Curdles said with a hint of menace. "You got one week, Winchester." He moved in closer. "One. If I don't have one hundred and fifty gold on my desk in one week, I'll have me a pet dragon living in a little aquarium."

"Ninety-five, you mean."

"Nope, I don't mean ninety-five. One fifty. One week." Curdles pointed to an empty spot over by a credenza. "Or there will be a little glass home right there for you. Got it?"

Winchester looked over at the table. It sat directly under a wind vent and that god-awful painting of Curdles's mother. The thought of living under her constant sneer was enough to make him shiver.

"Got it," Winchester said with a gulp.

"Good." Curdles motioned at Zooks. "Take our friend here out back and give his tail a little snip."

"Wait!" Winchester said, looking over Zook's thumb. "If he cuts off my tail the vertebrae won't grow back."

"Lizards get their tails back," Curdles said. He held up a book entitled *Caring For Your New Pet Lizard* and tapped the cover. "I've been reading up."

"You can read?"

Curdles frowned. "Don't push me, Winchester. The tail will grow back. Your head won't."

"The bones *won't* grow back," Winchester exclaimed. "Instead, it'll fill in with a cartilaginous tube."

"So?"

"So I could suffer from phantom-limb syndrome and that

would not make for a great pet. I would be quite cantankerous indeed."

"Fine," Curdles said, looking like he didn't want to be one-upped. "Have him tell you where to snip from," he said to Zooks. "We wouldn't want our little Snoogums to be grumpy all the time."

"Snoogums?"

"Oh yeah." Curdles smiled. "That's what I'm going to name you when you become my pet."

"Snoogums?"

# AOPOW STATION

*A*opow Station was one of the larger portal hubs.
The structure was massive. There were rows of stores and restaurants reaching so far that they were just barely in sight. Its smooth walls moved into a high arching ceiling that had numerous indentations carrying miles of cabling and pipes. The grounds were equally detailed in their etchings and layout, though much of it was covered with grime. It wasn't one of the more cared-for stations.

"Wow," Bekner said reverently. "I've not seen the likes of this before."

"We are in a portal hub, gentlemen," said Whizzfiddle. "Aopow, to be exact."

"Is this what wizards does?" Gungren asked.

Whizzfiddle ignored him and glanced around. It had been some time since he'd traveled the systems and portal nodes had a way of moving around. There was no sense in ending up surrounded by werewolves or trolls, so he studied the map to be sure he knew where they were headed.

"I don't mean to bother you, Master Whizzfiddle..." Orophin whispered.

"I do so appreciate it."

"It's just that there seems to be some interest in our arrival."

The elderly wizard dipped his head under the directory podium and took inventory of other travelers. Sure enough, there were a few scrags closing in on Whizzfiddle's position.

Scrags always littered the Aopow hub, and local authorities did little to prevent them, which was primarily because there was no local authority in Aopow. Many people carried weapons to ward off the scrags, but wizards weren't known for their weaponry, and magic was rendered moot in this particular hub due to something called an electrical variance. Whizzfiddle never bothered to learn the ins and outs, he just knew that even attempting to light a pipe with an incantation would prove futile.

"Bekner," Whizzfiddle said as he refocused on the podium, "we may have need of your size here."

"I ain't got a weapon."

Whizzfiddle craned his neck. "My good dwarf, you *are* a weapon."

Zel slipped behind Beckner.

"Especially after those beans you ate at lunch," added Orophin.

Zel jumped out from behind Beckner and squatted beside Gungren instead. Whizzfiddle shook his head.

"Enough out of you, elf," Beckner said.

"I don't need you to actually attack the scrags—"

"The what?" Gungren said.

"Scrags. That's what they call the portal thugs. Anyway, I don't need you to attack them, but I need some time to learn the maps before we exit the portal. So, act menacing or something."

Bekner began cracking his knuckles as Whizzfiddle resumed his search.

He traced the thin colored lines that ran from station to station, searching for Dakmenhem. With all the overlying routes, each having its own color except where they ran together, it was a tricky proposition. Number 219 looked to be the ticket. Whizzfiddle began carefully spinning the dials. He took his time since they were known to stick if handled too roughly.

"The scrags are getting closer," Zel squeaked.

"I just need another minute or so."

"I don't think we're after having another minute, wizard," Beckner replied.

"Why we just not go?" said Gungren.

"Because it takes proper handling to do these things."

"Why?"

"Because you have to set the dials to the location you're going to."

"Why?"

"Because each number represents a portal and if you don't input the proper sequence you'll end up somewhere you didn't intend."

"Why?"

"Because that's how it was designed."

"Why?"

"I don't know why!"

"Um…Master Whizzfiddle…" Orophin said, pointing at the scrags, who were about twenty feet away and closing in quickly.

"I don't get the trouble," Gungren said as he reached out a stubby finger, pressing the green button. "Just hit this one."

"No!"

# THE UPDATE

*T*reneth of Dahl hated loose ends. He wanted nothing more than to gain a seat on the council, and eventually gain the council's chair, but a very close second was the disbarment of his former master. Once Treneth took on a project, he saw it through.

And that meant he had to put another call in to Teggins.

"My boys spotted them in Aopow Station," Teggins said through the TalkyThingy.

"So they've been delayed, then?"

"Kind of."

"Kind of?"

"They fled to Gorgan before my guys could shake them down."

"Why would they go to Gorgan?"

"How the hell am I supposed to know, Treneth?" Teggins answered. "All I know is that they're off the grid now so getting back to Kek is going to take them a while."

"Fine," Treneth responded. "I will make the arrangements to have your case reviewed with the council, Teggins. Once that is done, we will be even again."

"Yeah, even," Teggins said, followed by a click and a solid tone.

Now that Whizzfiddle and his quest was sufficiently tied up, Treneth could keep his focus on other matters.

The plan would begin tonight and the first step would be getting Muppy alone. The biggest hurdle toward that goal was it being Friday night.

Friday evenings were the notorious party night for wizards. Many would be partaking in drink, dancing, and various forms of debauchery. Muppy was known for being in the middle of that mix.

It was doubtful that another party at the Croomplatt twins' estate was planned, seeing as how the Croomplatts had just managed an event the week prior.

Zotrinder wouldn't be with her. The elf tended to play dress-up at the end of the week in a manner that made him look more like a woman than most women felt comfortable with, mainly because he looked better than the majority of them.

Ibork, too, was out of the question. Muppy despised the halfling. Who didn't? Aside from Treneth, Ibork was the least favored wizard in Rangmoon.

So Treneth just had to get to her before she set out on the town.

He judged the time to be nearing five o'clock. The partying didn't begin until well past nine.

He had time to prepare. He would scrub his hands and fingernails until they were flawless. It would be an arduous enough task to convince Muppy that he was seeing her purely socially. To arrive with hands gloved would be evidenced as business to her. He would be cleaned, clipped, filed, dressed smoothly, and carrying forth an air of change and personal interest in the council chairperson.

Rimpertuz would play his part as well, though he

wouldn't understand his role until it was beyond repair. Even if he had misgivings, his apprentice would comply so as to avoid the wrath of his master. After all, the man did say that he would do anything to garner forgiveness.

Ah, the beauty of creative thought. *This*, Treneth mused, *is how a wizard* should *play the game of magic.*

"Rimpertuz," he called out, "that is enough for now."

His apprentice set the shovel aside, closed up the barrel and dragged it over to the rest of the heap, and then approached Treneth.

"I shall need you to shower and dress nicely, Rimpertuz," he said. "You are going to run an errand for me."

"Yes, sir," Rimpertuz muttered, wiping the sweat from his brow.

"Now, now," Treneth said, "we had agreed that you would not take a sour attitude toward your debt."

"No, sir."

"Good," Treneth said. "Oh, what happened with Idoon?"

Rimpertuz brightened.

"He says it'll be on the road first thing tomorrow even if he has to personally pick each pea pod and load it himself."

*Money may not be able to buy love*, Treneth thought, *but it sure can afford satisfaction.* That shipment would serve to solidify another challenge for Whizzfiddle. If the old wizard did somehow manage to get to Kek, Peapod Pecklesworthy would be far too busy shucking pods to be worried about anything else. Addiction was a powerful thing.

"Well done, Rimpertuz," Treneth said. "I daresay you will make an impression on Master Pecklesworthy indeed. You did sign your name to the shipment, yes?"

Rimpertuz's face fell. Treneth hadn't expected the man to think of such a thing, but it would have been a nice touch on solidifying that Rimpertuz had acted on his own.

"No matter, my apprentice. I'm certain that Farmer Idoon will reveal your name when Master Pecklesworthy asks."

Again, Treneth reveled in his own ingenuity.

"Yes, sir. That's a good point."

"Those are the only kind of points I make, Rimpertuz."

"Where am I going for this errand, sir?"

"Hmmm? Oh, yes, well, I'm having you carry a message to the council chair."

Rimpertuz's eyes opened considerably. "Councilwoman Muppy, sir?"

"That's correct," Treneth said, tilting his head. "Is that an issue?"

"No, sir," the apprentice replied. "Not at all, sir. I'll get showered quickly, sir."

"Thoroughly, Rimpertuz," he called after his departing apprentice.

"Well," he continued, talking to an approaching ostrich, "this may end up easier than I'd anticipated."

The ostrich crackled in response.

"Agreed," Treneth said, nodding his head. "Agreed."

# GORGAN

*G*organ was a massive land. It had to be to fit the size of its inhabitants. The smallest gorgan Whizzfiddle could recall was still larger than the largest giant he'd ever seen.

Various texts described how a group of wizards remodeled this area of Ononokin as a testament to the power of combined transfigurations. In one particular historical recollection, notes in the margin pointed out how the newly grown gorgans accidentally stomped out the wizards as they ran around looking for giant fig leaves to cover themselves up with.

The trees stood hundreds of feet tall and the shrubbery were tens of feet high. It was often too much for the average mind to accept, so Whizzfiddle just pretended the shrubs were the trees and the trees were a figment of his imagination. It worked for him.

"Well done, Gungren," Whizzfiddle said in a nasty tone. "Your recklessness has just landed us in one of the most dangerous places in the Upperworld."

Gungren kicked at the dirt as Bekner patted him on the shoulder reassuringly. "I not do it on purpose."

"Oh? Did the button press itself, then?"

"No."

"No," Whizzfiddle agreed, "it didn't. You did, and now we are in the land of the *real* giants until the portal activates again."

"Real giants?" Orophin asked, his face holding a look of awe.

"Yes," Whizzfiddle said as he rummaged through his bag to top off a mug of ale. "Not the fifteen-footers like Gungren here should be, but the thirty-to-forty footers that have a standing rule when they see any little biped: kill it."

Whizzfiddle drank deeply, letting the power flow through his veins. He kept his eyes closed and counted silently to ten and back down again.

He wasn't even a day into this adventure and things were already falling apart. It had to be him. Every quest he'd ever been a part of ran into all sorts of difficulties. Even the small ones.

He recalled one assignment where all he had to do was help a child find a lost doll. It had taken two weeks and a trip to Flaymtahk Island, which meant he had to cross the ocean, and he so despised the ocean. Then he had picked his way through Kesper's Range, traveled through Dahl, where he was coerced by Treneth's parents to take the young man on as an apprentice, then through Metrian, and finally back to the child's home in Argan. He had nothing to show for his journey other than a few scars and a feeling of unmitigated failure. As Whizzfiddle arrived, the child came running outside with the doll in hand, saying it had been under her bed the whole time. The parents explained that she had found it only minutes after Whizzfiddle had left to begin the quest and that they had no way to get a hold of him.

"We'll be here for weeks," Whizzfiddle hissed.

He sighed and took another shot of ale. Who knew that a simple dolly-quest could have wreaked so much havoc in a wizard's life, and have such far-reaching consequences?

"Yes, Zel," Whizzfiddle said, sensing Zel's hand was up.

"Did you say weeks, sir?"

"That's what I said. It could be weeks. A portal doesn't stay open after you use it. Something to do with charging, or whatever. I'm not a technician."

"That doesn't make any sense," Orophin said. "Certainly a lot of people use these things."

"Portal locations are on the power grid," said Whizzfiddle. "So when you land, it is immediately recharged. But that's in the Underworld. Most of the Upperworld ones are hidden, as you may recall when we searched for the one outside of Rangmoon. These require more time to recharge." He pointed at a set of shiny squares that sat on top of the portal. "These things collect the rays of the sun, or something like that. Again, I'm not technical."

"Can we force it open?" Bekner said.

"I've never known anyone that could," Whizzfiddle replied. "Even if you could, it may not have enough juice to get us back anyway."

"You could," Gungren said.

"I could what?"

"Use magic to make portal have juice."

"Hmmph."

Theoretically, that was true. But no matter how many spells he had tried to get the blasted portals opened after they'd shut down, he had never succeeded. Typically, he would just sag to the ground, thank The Twelve for giving him enough foresight to pack extra ale and foodstuffs, and then he'd lay low for a while. The problem was that he had only a month to accomplish this mission or he faced a long time of watching others practice magic while he stood on the sidelines.

Whizzfiddle turned his back on them and dug into his pack for another helping of ale and an apple.

Idoon's apples were the best and they always seemed to bring him some calm. He would have sworn that they were enhanced with something pleasant. Idoon always gave away the first apple, then you had to start paying for them. Worth every silver, Whizzfiddle thought as he chewed.

His brain ached from all this thinking and working, but he had to come up with options.

They could walk out, but that would be a trying expedition.

The Gorgan Mountains were a good hundred miles away and they were huge and crawling with creatures large enough for gorgans to call pets.

Beyond the mountains lay the Modan Republic, and that was not a place for sane people to travel. Looking around, he decided that sanity may not be much of a deterrent. Modan had a unique water supply system that kept everyone smiling. Actually, it would prove an interesting place for Whizzfiddle to spend the remainder of his years if he lost his guild status.

They could keep to the coast and get as far as Natix, but that would take longer than just waiting for the portal to reengage, and they'd likely get hit by highwaymen along the way.

The fact was that, beyond waiting it out, they had little choice.

It was going to be dark soon. Animals would start looking for a way to feed. He would have to cast a spell of protection. He just wondered over whom the spell of protection was worthy.

"What is that?" Orophin said.

"It looks like a finger or something," Bekner replied.

Whizzfiddle tried to ignore them as he thought of options.

He could try casting a flame on the shiny top of the portal. If the squares got their charge from the heat of the sun, that may be all that was required. It was one thing he'd thought about before but had never tried.

"That a nail, yep."

"Aye, lad, it is."

He remembered why it wouldn't work. The sun's heat was tempered due to the distance and protection from the atmosphere. If Whizzfiddle put a magical flame on the portal it'd just melt, and he didn't have the wherewithal to hold a constant low-grade heat over a few hours.

"If that's a nail…" Orophin started.

"…then it must be a finger," Zel finished.

"That's after being a big finger."

Whizzfiddle really wished that this questing party would just shut up and give him time to think. Here they were in the middle of a predicament and all they could talk about was some gigantic finger.

"Oh damn," he said as he bolted up and dived toward Gungren, dragging him away from the monstrous digit.

He pushed them all back.

"You do not sneak up on a gorgan, Gungren," Whizzfiddle said in a whisper, the words nearly twisting in on themselves. "Even at your fullest height you'd be but a child compared to that thing. Our best course of action would be to move swiftly and silently away."

"Who up der?" a booming voice sounded.

Whizzfiddle hushed them all.

"Somebody up der?"

Swinging his arm in a circle and pointing, Whizzfiddle

guided them all to the closest grouping of dense foliage he could find.

"Sound like little people," the voice said. "I not hurt little people. I need help."

"Damn," Whizzfiddle said, stopping in his tracks.

There was nothing worse than the sound of a gorgan in distress. In all their hugeness, they were as innocent as children at heart. The only reason they killed the "little people" these days was because gorgans were somewhat of a sport for other races. Fealty quests nearly always involved gorgans or dragons (which gorgans referred to as "widdle birdies wif big teef dat burped fire"), or both. So they had learned to be vicious. But when an agreement of peace was in place, they were as gentle as butterflies, and not those butterflies the Hubintegler gnomes in the Underworld genetically spliced with crocodiles, either.

"Please?"

The elderly wizard slunk to the finger and found it bent at a ninety-degree angle. He peered over the edge and was met with brown eyes the size of ponds.

"Hello, little people," the gorgan said. "I named Nern."

"Nern," Whizzfiddle said with a nod. "It seems you are in a bit of a predicament."

"If that mean Nern in trouble, dat about right."

The cliff face was bumpy, offering many ledges for Nern to grip and gather himself on. Sadly, gorgans weren't all that bright and the drop was too steep for the gorgan to survive.

"Use magic," Gungren said, causing Whizzfiddle to jump and nearly join the gorgan in his exigency.

"You know," Whizzfiddle said, poking Gungren in the chest, "you're starting to draw on my last nerve."

"Hello, little people," Nern said to Gungren.

"I not little always," Gungren said. "Just in bad spot now."

"Nern in bad spot too."

"Yep."

Within minutes they were all looking for solutions to Nern's situation. Orophin pointed out a sundry of ways that the gorgan could climb up but they all relied on the ability to convey delicate information to a gorgan.

"Use magic," Gungren repeated.

"It may come to that, yes," Whizzfiddle said. "A wizard uses magic only as a final resort. Nern, I think I know how we can help you."

"Nern will save them lives if them save Nern's," the gorgan said desperately.

Whizzfiddle shooed everyone away and looked down at Nern. Not many people could say that about a thirty-foot creature.

"Okay, Nern," Whizzfiddle said, "you see that ledge right there?"

He pointed and Nern nodded.

"Can you put your foot on it?"

Nern did.

"Excellent! Now, can you put your other hand up here, next to me?"

Nern slammed his hand up, practically knocking the wizard from his feet.

Whizzfiddle backed away and shouted, "Okay, Nern, pull yourself up."

"I not know what you mean."

Whizzfiddle itched at his beard and looked about. He reached into his backpack and pulled out a large apple. He approached the edge.

"Ooh," said Nern, "a grape!"

Close enough.

"Do you like grapes?"

"Yep, and I hungry now."

"Would you like to see more grapes, Nern?"

Nern smiled widely. Whizzfiddle went back to his backpack and dumped all the apples onto the ground.

"There are a lot of app...grapes up here," he said.

A loud grunt signaled that Nern was pulling himself up. He had himself pushed up to his waist, his arms fully locked in position on the cliff's edge, revealing a crisp white shirt with a tight collar and a dark, patterned vest that was left unbuttoned. Gorgans were known to have a sense of style.

"Woah, he got a big head," Gungren said.

Coming from a giant, that was saying something.

"Indeed," Whizzfiddle said. "You should all get clear, just in case."

"What Nern do now?"

"Ah, well, as to that...just step up, Nern."

Nern frowned as he looked around. "Huh?"

"Astonishing," Orophin said with just a hint of sarcasm.

Obviously, Whizzfiddle was going to have to come up with a different plan.

## A TROUBLED BUSINESS

*W*inchester's tail was a bit tender as he strolled into the studio.

If he had found fifty reliable people to work with, his magazine would have been on the presses by now and his tail would still be intact. As it was, reliability cost more than he could afford. That meant he got ogres. Ten of them. They did as they were told well enough. The issue was, though, that they were not self-starters. This translated into a bunch of mindless wandering in an attempt to look busy. Sometimes they even took shifts drifting about.

"Oknot," Winchester said to the closest ogre, "lift me up to my pedestal, if you would."

Oknot did so and, obviously knowing the routine, clapped his hands. "Decision man here!"

Everyone gathered around.

Another issue working with this lot was that they all acted as if they were in charge as well. Actually, they refused to be considered less than anyone on an organizational chart. They certainly weren't fond of the term "boss," unless they were referred to by the same moniker. If they were working for a crime boss, though, they seemed to revel in calling the boss "boss."

"As you all know," Winchester said, "we are not yet profitable. That means we're going to have to make some hard choices. Yes, Blerg?"

"We is, or you is?"

"I is...will."

"Got it," Blerg said. "Go on."

"Thank you, Blerg," Winchester said. "If we don't get this magazine done and shipped soon, everyone is going to be out of a job."

"We is, or you is?"

"All of us is...are," Winchester said.

"Got it."

"So what we need is a really hot model who will do nudes."

He looked at the two females on staff. Neither fit the mold he was looking for.

"*PlayDragon* can be a reality," he continued. "Each of us can be sitting in the lap of luxury. Our pockets can be loaded with gold and our plates will never be empty." He cast his best dragon gaze around. "We have to work together to make it happen."

Oknot stepped up. "How we do it?"

"We have to find a good-looking orc female."

"But we try this and it not ever happen. Been long time."

"Yes," Winchester agreed. "The problem there is that I've been spending all of my time setting up deals and getting layouts and equipment ready. I need to go on the hunt and find that special lady. All it takes is one and we'll be in business."

"So, what we do, then?"

"Oknot," Winchester said, "get this place cleaned up. Spotless. The rest of you help him set everything just right, except you three." He pointed at Blerg, Qayla, and Patty. "Blerg, you're going to be the muscle that gets me into LaHott tonight."

"Got it."

"Qayla and Patty, you two get dolled up as best you can. You'll be walking in with me as my eye candy."

"Qayla not having candy," Patty said in a voice deeper than Blerg's. "Gives her gas."

"Right," Winchester said. "Let's just say that you two will be my dates for the night."

"Oh," Patty said, eyebrows raised. "Okay, but no funny stuff on first date."

"Funny stuff good with me," Qayla argued as they walked toward the dressing room.

"No, it not, Qayla," Patty was saying as they rounded the corner. "You need grow you self-steamer and stop using your body."

Winchester climbed down and trotted off to his study, barely dodging all the bustling ogre and troll feet. He pushed through the small flap in the door and scurried up to his tiny desk.

Everything was mapped out. Articles were written by local talent. It wasn't cheap, but it would be worth it. Most subscribers would look at the pictures and ignore the articles; most subscribers wouldn't be able to read the articles anyway. But Winchester felt that having hard-hitting journalism fill the pages in conjunction with the nudes would attract even highbrow consumers, or at least give plausible deniability for why they purchased such a publication.

He thumbed through the layouts. The look was far from perfect, but it would do fine for the first issue. But it wouldn't matter how good or bad it looked if there was no cover model.

"Orc-next-door type," he said to his empty office.

He had worked on getting Yultza from Curdles's clan, but to no avail. Under all her armor and weaponry was the perfect specimen for *PlayDragon*. Winchester had never seen beyond the armor, but he could tell by the way she moved. And her face was flawless, as far as orcs go.

Yultza's response to the suggestion had been to pluck Winchester across the room. His back ached for days.

At this point he would have to settle for a less-than-perfect specimen.

The stash of gold was almost depleted. Ten shiny discs were all that remained. After tonight there would be half that, or it would start doubling exponentially.

Tomorrow morning, Winchester Hargrath Jr. III would either be on his way to the top, or he would be a lizard on the run.

# THE DATE

*F*reshly scrubbed and wearing his best suit, Treneth stood patiently at the entrance to The Watchtower Restaurant. It was the only place elegant enough on the west coast of Ononokin for one of his stature.

"May I seat you, sir?" the host said, offering his hand in greeting.

Treneth pulled his hand back, not wanting to have this young man suddenly interested in courting him. Treneth had smeared magical elixir on his hands so that when Muppy touched him she would find him irresistible. It would affect anyone who touched him, though, so he had to be cautious. It would not do her any harm in any way, of course, nor would it affect her judgment over doing things considered untoward. The amount of alcohol she regularly imbibed would, and likely had, led her down paths of debauchery that Treneth could only shudder at, but this elixir was only a temporary means of making her not find him disgusting. By the time they were done with dinner, the spell would wear off and she would be left with her normal wits, though they would likely be impaired with wine by then. Again, Muppy was known for getting sloshed in a fashion suited to typical wizards, and that would play into Treneth's plans perfectly.

"Momentarily," he replied. "I am waiting for someone."

The host bowed politely and walked back to his podium as Treneth inhaled deeply. His stomach threatened to growl as he saw a tray of sizzling steak and roasted potatoes cross the room. If nothing else, he was in for a decent meal.

A few minutes later Rimpertuz appeared at the door, opening it wide for Councilwoman Muppy. She curtsied and giggled at Treneth's apprentice. Then she saw Treneth and frowned.

*No matter*, he thought. *I'm just the warm-up.*

"Madam," he said, offering his hand.

She leaned backwards, bumping into a delighted Rimpertuz.

Treneth did his best to look injured. "They have been thoroughly washed, I assure you."

"I'll pass, Treneth," Muppy replied. "So this stud…"—she coughed lightly—"student of yours says that you wanted to meet me for dinner?"

"I feel that there has been much negativity between us, and—"

"I'm here and I'm hungry." She then looked him over carefully. "Is this a date, Treneth?"

Treneth felt his cheeks burning. "No...I mean, well..."

Muppy shrugged.

"Fine with me," she said. "Just means you're paying." She then moved to the podium. "Dear boy," she said to the host, "how is your mom faring these days?"

"She is better, madam. I thank you for asking."

"Wonderful," Muppy said, patting the young man's hand. "She is such a dear lady. My usual table, if you would. Oh,"— she turned to wink at Treneth—"and do bring a bottle of your best."

Treneth looked at Rimpertuz and pointed at the door.

"I'll take it from here, my apprentice. Not to worry now, you'll be happier at the end of this night than I will be, and it won't cost you nearly as much as it will me…at least not monetarily."

"Sir?"

"You'll see soon enough. At precisely midnight, you will meet me at Muppy's estate. Do not be late."

Muppy had already finished half a glass as Treneth pulled up his chair. He feigned to trip and glanced his hand across her forearm.

At first she looked at her arm, horrified. Then her eyes began to cloud and her face relaxed.

Suddenly, she was all agleam.

He felt pride as Muppy's visage changed from disgust to one of a woman in lust. Treneth was not an average man who would easily succumb to womanly charms. *Dream all you want, my dear*, he thought, *for tonight your downfall begins*.

"What does that look mean?" Muppy said.

Treneth blanched. "I don't know what you're talking about." He quickly grabbed his menu.

"I never knew you had such a crush on me, Treneth of Dahl."

Muppy had never gotten his name right before. At least not on purpose. And a crush? The thought sickened him. She was attractive enough, sure. That wasn't the problem. It was her throw-in with the lifestyle of the other wizards. Unacceptable at best and certainly not suiting for one of his caliber. But, plans were plans. Besides, it was just the elixir talking.

"Let's just say that I am one who is full of surprises, Councilwoman."

"We're on a date, Treneth," she said, waving her hand. "No formalities. Call me by my name."

JOHN P. LOGSDON & CHRISTOPHER P. YOUNG

"Yes, of course."

"Go ahead." She winked at him as she drained the glass and began to refill it. "I want to hear it."

"Muppy," he said shakily.

She giggled and pushed the bottle of wine toward him.

Her reaction was stronger than he'd expected. She loathed him. Everyone loathed him. The elixir was potent indeed!

"I wanted to talk to you about something guild-related."

"No business on a date, Treneth."

"It's just a minor point and it would make me feel quite a bit better about...loosening up."

She sighed and motioned him to go ahead.

"There is a friend of mine from the Underworld," he said, pouring more wine in her glass. "His name is Teggins. You may know of him."

"Yep."

"Well, he has served a number of years' sentence and is looking to regain his travel status."

"And?"

"You know how particular I am with details, madam...Muppy," he said with a smile. "I believe the man is repentant and has studied well enough to be readmitted."

"That's it?"

"That is indeed it."

"Okay," she said, taking another sip. "Just have the papers on my desk Monday and I'll sign the release."

"Actually, I happen to have them right here. If you wouldn't mind?"

"Fine," she said a bit testily before taking the pen and signing.

"Excellent," Treneth said. "I will drop these by the offices and put them in for Agnitine to register."

Muppy reached out and touched his hand. *Unfathomable*, he thought.

"Let's talk about something else," she purred. "What kind of fun are we going to have tonight, Treneth of Dahl?"

"Oh, dear."

## AIDING A GORGAN

"Nern," Whizzfiddle said to the extraordinary creature, "you seem like a bright chap to me."

"It true."

"I'll tell you what I'm going to do."

"Okay."

Whizzfiddle began walking backwards, his voice rising slightly with each step. "I'm going to show you how to get over that wall."

"Nern like that." He stopped smiling. "And Nern save your life too," he continued, looking at each of them in turn. "Nern made promise."

"You know what a secret is…right, Nern?"

"Of course Nern know. Nern not dumb."

"Indeed." Whizzfiddle chuckled. "I have a secret, but…see those little people over there?"

"Yep."

"They don't know the secret," Whizzfiddle said, his throat getting a little tender. "That's why I'm standing way back here."

"Why they not know?"

"Because, Nern, it's a *gorgan* secret."

Nern's eyes widened considerably. "It is?"

"Yes, sir," Whizzfiddle replied. "I learned it once when I was here helping...um...well, you wouldn't know him."

"Boomreck?"

"You know Boomreck, then?"

The name was familiar, but it had been a few hundred years. And with gorgans, names like Boomreck, Roombeck, Kemboor, or—Whizzfiddle's personal favorite—Kerboom, were commonplace.

"Everyone know Boomreck. He work with some little people before. Dat you?"

"Possibly," he said with a shrug. "Either way, I know the secret. But I can't let the other little people know a gorgan secret, can I?"

"No, dat would be bad."

"I *could* tell you, of course."

"Dat make sense, yep."

"Although..." Whizzfiddle tapped his foot as if he were thinking it through.

"What wrong?"

"It's just that I remember promising that I wouldn't say anything to anyone."

"Like you say, I are gorgan, so it okay."

"That's the thing," Whizzfiddle said. "Boomreck—if that's the same gorgan I was working with all those years ago—well, he didn't specify."

"Boomreck understand. Boomreck know Nern keep gorgan secret in brain box."

Which was their equivalent of a safety-deposit box. There was plenty of room for secrets since not much else filled the space.

"Hmmm," Whizzfiddle said, still acting unsure. "I suppose—"

"It okay," Nern said with a hint of exasperation. "Nern getting tired."

"Oh, all right," Whizzfiddle said, "but you make sure you keep this secret secure or I'll come and give you a walloping you won't soon forget."

"Yes, sir," Nern said, looking truly frightened.

"Fine, fine. Come over here and I'll tell you."

Nern jumped over the ledge and took two steps to where Whizzfiddle was and then plopped himself down as if preparing for a tale. Whizzfiddle pulled himself back to his feet and brushed the dirt from his robe and then slapped Nern on his gigantic knee.

"You did it, Nern!"

"Did what?"

Whizzfiddle watched Nern's face slowly contort. It was as though the tiniest flame seemed to light from a candle atop an old chest of drawers covered with cobwebs sitting in the deep recesses of Nern's childish mind. Nern inhaled quickly and jumped back up, again knocking Whizzfiddle off his feet, and did a rather large dance. Whizzfiddle rolled away as deftly as possible.

"Nern did it! Nern did it!"

Then he stopped.

"Hey, wait," he said to Whizzfiddle. "Der no secret, is der?"

Whizzfiddle grinned and shook his head.

"You smart for a little people," Nern said.

"All in a day's work," Whizzfiddle replied with a wink.

The gorgan released a booming laugh. "Thank you for help," Nern said, looking over all of them. "Now it Nern turn to save you."

He began briskly walking away.

Orophin looked as confused as the rest of them. Whizzfiddle just shook his head.

"How are you going to save us, Nern?" the elf called out.

"I leaving," Nern called back. "If Nern stay with little people, Nern have to kill little people. It gorgan way."

"He a dumb one," Gungren said.

"Aye, lad. He is at that."

"It's quite logical, if you think about it," Whizzfiddle countered. "Either way, our friend Nern has done something that could help us, though I don't know how."

They all looked in the direction Whizzfiddle was gazing. The portal had popped back open. The lights were dimmed, but being open gave the wizard a chance to power it up for a trip back to the hub.

"I thought you said—" Orophin began.

"I did," Whizzfiddle said, cutting him off. "It must be his size. You saw how he kept knocking me off my feet with all his bouncing around."

"So now we can get after getting back?" Bekner said.

"It will take a little ingenuity, but at least we've got a chance now."

Whizzfiddle grabbed the hood on Gungren's robe.

"Oh no," he said. "You'll be staying away from that unit until I say we're ready to go. Bekner, if you would be so kind as to keep an eye on our little tinkerer, I would be obliged. Zel, if you would be so kind as to watch Bekner, I would be obliged to you as well. Orophin, I could use some of that elvish inventiveness, if you're game."

"He is," the others chorused.

Orophin put his hands on his hips. "He said *game*, you idiots."

## AM I ALONE?

*M*uppy's bed shifted.

She slowly opened her eyes.

A light groan next to her confirmed that she was not alone.

The previous night was a little foggy, as were most Friday nights. Muppy had never woken up with an unknown in her bed, though. Unknown earlier in the evening, certainly; well-known by the next morning.

She looked at the full-length mirror across the room. It reflected a body next to her. Plus, there were a pair of men's trousers on the chair beside the mirror. Blue with thin striping. She had definitely seen them before but couldn't place to whom they belonged.

She reached down to verify she was wearing a nightgown. She was. It was the one with the frilly lace that rode high on her thighs.

It must have been an interesting evening.

She concentrated and the previous night's events started coming back.

The date with Treneth, the wine, the wonderful chicken

with mushrooms and lemon sauce, the...nothing. She couldn't remember much beyond that except vague shadows.

She suddenly grew nauseous.

Treneth of Dahl was in her bed?

She vowed off wine and determined that she would have to burn the bedding, have the house fumigated, quarantine the room and move to the opposite side of the house...hell, she would likely just sell the house and relocate across town.

Taking a deep breath, she craned her neck far enough to catch a glimpse of him.

She took a deep breath, afraid that reality would match the nightmare.

Then she blinked.

"Rimpertuz?"

# GUNGREN TINKERS

*hizzfiddle* awoke to the sound of crunching leaves.

Bekner was walking back into the clearing, carrying something under his arm. It looked like a copy of the *Rangmoonian Times*. Zel grabbed the paper and found his way into the woods next.

Whizzfiddle was propped up against a tree and his back ached nearly as much as his head. Even if he wasn't aging at the same rate others did, he was still in his 600s and his body considered itself in retirement.

Orophin was fast asleep with his head resting nicely in a bed of leaves. Elves knew how to get comfortable in the forest.

Gungren was busily working on the portal.

Whizzfiddle pulled his flask out to drink his morning medicine. It was empty.

Every bone cracked, creaked, or did both as he stretched. Aging slowly or not, he was getting old.

Maybe it *was* time to settle into a life of leisure. Well,

more than usual anyway. He had enough money to last him, even with taxes and alms to the poor. And farming wasn't *that* bad, especially if you hired laborers to do the actual farming for you. The magic would be missed. Direly missed. Plus, he would have to swear off the juice or his body would suffer the constant ache of power.

Whizzfiddle looked at the empty flask. The first step is admitting you have a problem, they always told him. He did have a problem. He couldn't get enough. Yes, he was addicted to the booze, but that wasn't the issue. It was the power that was the real addiction. Any wizard would support him in this. There was nothing more magical than the flow of power, even if said power was used to do magic.

No, this was his life. A little work, but mostly play. Play without booze, without magic, was not play. It was too intellectual. Debate and deep discussions were a fine diversion, just not for the rest of his life.

This just meant that...

"Gungren!" Whizzfiddle said, springing to his feet. "What in the name of The Twelve do you think you're doing?"

Gungren seemed to ignore the weight of the protest.

"I are fixing the box, master."

"I thought I was very clear that you were to stay away from that box?" Whizzfiddle said while wagging his finger. "And quit calling me that."

"Sorry, master."

Bekner was standing behind them as Orophin stirred from his slumber.

"You were supposed to watch him, Bekner."

"When nature's after calling, wizard, you oblige."

"It almost working," Gungren said as he continued tinkering. "I got it figured too."

The lights were on, which was something Whizzfiddle had not been able to accomplish all night. It wasn't as though the runt could make things much worse, aside from completely destroying the portal. He grunted, shrugged and went for his backpack. Years of practice told him that a little essence in his veins would bring clarity.

Moving back to the portal, he watched Gungren's fat fingers as they poked and prodded a bunch of wires behind the unit. Gungren was using his nails to slice through some of them.

"Zel," Orophin said with a yawn as Zel returned from his morning meditation, "mind?"

Zel handed him the paper and Orophin scampered off into the woods.

"Gungren…" Whizzfiddle started, afraid that the matrix of connections the tiny giant was working on would only serve to hinder them further.

"Just a minute," Gungren said.

"You do realize—"

"Just a minute," Gungren said again.

"—that you have—"

Gungren groaned. "Which word have you wondering? I trying to work."

Whizzfiddle raised his eyebrows and looked at Bekner, who merely shrugged. Gungren resumed, shaking his head and mumbling.

Bekner pulled Whizzfiddle and Zel away.

"Ye think ye'll get us back to what we were?" Bekner asked. "It's no life for a dwarf to be this be big." He looked at his arms and legs. Then he rubbed his chin. "I can't even grow a proper beard."

"I'm sure you can also imagine that a knight in my situation is, sir, a little frustrating."

Knowing how his own situation was precarious, Whizzfiddle did understand. He patted Zel on the shoulder.

"It fixed," Gungren announced as Orophin returned.

Gungren finished putting the back panel on and stepped around front with the rest of them.

The lights were all on and there was a faint humming sound.

"Well done, Gungren," Whizzfiddle said, amazed. "Well done, indeed."

"It no problem."

"Now," Orophin said, "we just have to hope that whatever he did still gets us to the hub and doesn't turn us into something worse than what we already are."

"Aye."

"That not happen."

"It's all about trust, gentlemen," said Whizzfiddle.

"You're after trusting that Gungren knows what he was doing, then?"

"Not in the slightest, no," Whizzfiddle replied heavily. "I refer to trusting that the universe will do what it will with us regardless of our best laid plans."

They stepped on the platform. There were no complex dials to contend with since the Gorgan portal was only connected to two hubs, Aopow and Wimat. Whizzfiddle turned the single lever to point to Wimat Station and then, with a smile, he motioned Gungren to press the green button.

Gungren reached out.

It fizzled.

It popped.

It whirred.

It went dim.

They were still standing in Gorgan. Whizzfiddle grunted and patted Gungren on the head, giving him points for at least trying.

"Sir," Zel said, barely above a whisper. "What about using magic to power it now that the lights are on?"

"Yes, yes," Whizzfiddle agreed. "I shall. I just do so despise using magic for such trivial things."

He emptied the flask, cast a spell, and motioned Gungren to try again.

# A SEAT, IF YOU PLEASE

*T*reneth repacked his fingernails, donned his gloves, grabbed the guild book of regulations, and skipped off to Muppy's estate. He'd never skipped a day in his life, but the mental ecstasy of what was to come was overwhelming.

The day was just beginning to brighten as Treneth came around to sit on a white picket bench in Muppy's garden.

She had a most deft gardener, by Treneth's estimation.

The bushes were trimmed at right angles near the walkway, rounded for balance at the corners; flowers poked about in a variety of shades and hues; the grass edgings were immaculately shaped; and the entire area smelled fresh and lovely, as long as Treneth kept his hands downwind.

He had considered waiting out front, but he knew how wizards thought. Sneaking out the back was their modus operandi.

It would be a pleasure catching her with her pants down, in a manner of speaking.

Treneth pulled out his pocketwatch and flicked back its golden cover. The timepiece had been a gift from his father

JOHN P. LOGSDON & CHRISTOPHER P. YOUNG

on the day that he had been handed off to Whizzfiddle for his apprenticeship. He had often desired to crush the watch to a pulp but decided there was no point in punishing an inanimate object for the proverbial hell that his former master had put him through.

Muppy burst out the back door, pulling Rimpertuz behind her as he hastened to button his shirt.

Right on time.

"Now listen," she was saying to Rimpertuz, "you were not here. Understand?"

"But—"

"No buts, Rimpertuz. You were *not* here and you've *never* been here."

Rimpertuz sagged. "I understand."

"Ah," Treneth said, striding up the walkway, "there you are, my apprentice."

"Oh shi—"

"Indeed," Treneth said, looking at his fingers. "I would say the term is a fitting one, Madam Councilwoman."

"You've set me up."

Treneth ignored the comment.

"I'm sure the esteemed chair of the Wizards' Guild Council is well aware of the rules concerning relations with apprentices?" Treneth pulled out the book of regulations and opened it to his bookmarked section. "My bookmark just happened to fall on the very page in question," he added with an astonished look. "That is a stroke of serendipity, wouldn't you say?"

"He's your apprentice—not mine."

"It says here that wizards and apprentices are disallowed to engage in any relations outside of the professional realm."

"Like I said, he's not my apprentice."

"True, true," Treneth said. "Well, then, I guess there is nothing further to be concerned with. Except..." He ran a gloved finger across the page. "Tsk, tsk." Treneth looked up sadly. "It seems that is not an acceptable defense, madam. There's a line entered in the margin, signed off by the current guild—including yourself—that removes that specificity."

"You bastard," Muppy said with a growl. "You brought that to the council just a few weeks ago. You knew you were going to do this!"

Treneth did his best to look taken aback, but on the inside his skipping continued.

"Madam," he said with feigned surprise, "I assure you that I was merely searching out my apprentice."

"Is that so?"

"I was worried. He is usually toiling in the fields much earlier than this."

"So the most logical place for you to search was my house?"

"That's correct. The events of last evening did rather suggest he could be here."

Muppy's eyes darted around and she turned to Rimpertuz. "Did anything happen between us last night?"

Rimpertuz looked at her and then at Treneth.

"Don't look at him," she said, grabbing Rimpertuz by his face. "Did anything happen last night?"

"I...I think so."

"You mean you don't know?"

"I would appreciate you not taking that tone with my apprentice," Treneth said. "Besides, madam, it appears that you do not know either."

She hissed and bared her teeth and then took a step toward Treneth. Her eyes had turned a terrifying shade of red.

"What do you want?" she asked, poking him in the chest.

He backed away, rubbing his sternum. She had quite a poke.

"I beg your pardon, madam. I find offense in this entire matter." He continued rubbing. "You are the one engaged in shady activities here. To include me as being part of your ilk—"

"What..."

She poked him again.

"Do..."

Another poke.

"You..."

Harder this time, and on the nose.

"Want?"

"A seat on the council!"

"Done."

Treneth gawked. He had taken weeks to build his discussion points, fully expecting a round of debate. Hours and hours went into building a veritable chess match of dialog, arguments, and counterarguments. Not being able to fully engage was disheartening.

Then again, she just agreed to giving him a seat on the council.

"Now,"—she poked him once more—"get off my property before I rip you to shreds."

"Very well," Treneth said as he tried to contain his mirth. "Come along, Rimpertuz. We have work—"

"He will be returned to you when I'm done with him."

Both Treneth and his apprentice turned in surprise.

"Get in the house, Rimpertuz," she said intensely, pointing at the door. "If I'm going to be charged for having relations with an apprentice, I'm damn well going to have relations with an apprentice."

# THE CENTERFOLD

*L*aHott hadn't exactly been teeming with ladies the night before.

As was Winchester's luck lately, it had been gentleman's night at the club, which meant the ladies stayed away. One plus was that he was able to save a gold on the cover charge; the other was that he'd found a model.

Tazdoreena was scrawny and a little long in the face, but she was willing to do nude photography. At this point that outweighed looks. If nothing else, she was an orc.

"Blerg," he said, "could you check on Oknot and make sure that all the cameras and lights are set up properly? I still have one more tweak to this layout before I'll be ready to start filming."

"Got it."

Try as he might, Winchester just couldn't bring the layout together. He had studied quite a few newspapers and magazines to see where the successes and failures were. Content may be king, but only if the content was clear and pleasantly laid out. He shrugged. It was far from perfect, but it would have to suffice for the first issue.

He put on his little red velvet robe, carefully tucked his wounded tail, and strolled out to the set.

This was his day.

"We gots a problem," Blerg said.

"Don't we always? What is it this time?"

Blerg motioned for Winchester to walk around the corner to the set.

He found Tazdoreena standing in the nude with a camera dangling around her neck. She truly wasn't centerfold material, at least not to his discerning eye. He could only hope that she would stand passable for the pages of *PlayDragon*.

"Good day, Tazdoreena," Winchester said.

"Yeah," she said with a grunt and then snapped a photo. "We going to do this shoot thing or what?"

"We are," he stated. "If you would just put the camera back on the tripod and move over to the bed, we'll get the fans and lighting going straightaway."

Tazdoreena looked confused.

"How am I supposed to do nude photography if I don't have a camera?"

"Pardon me?"

The ogres backed away. Winchester rolled his eyes.

"You said last night that you wanted me to do nude photography," Tazdoreena answered. "I thought it was weird, but I've been asked to do stranger things."

"Heh," he said, slapping his knee. "There has been a miscommunication. You are in the nude, yes?"

She looked down at herself and then back at him as if he were stupid.

"Right," said Winchester. "The photography we are to engage in is of *me* photographing *you* in the nude."

"So you're going to take pictures of me while you're nude?"

"What? No, no, no." He waved his hands. "You'll stay nude and lay yourself on that bed there, posing in various provocative ways, right?"

"Okay," she said at length.

"I'll stand over here with the camera and will give you directions as to how to move and what facial expressions to have. As you do this, I'll take photos for my new magazine."

"So you want me to be a nude *model*."

"I believe that's what I explained last evening."

"That changes everything," Tazdoreena said, snatching up her clothes. "Not doing it."

Winchester rushed over to Tazdoreena before she could get to the door.

"Is it the pay?"

"The pay?" she said, scoffing. "It's the principle. I'm not going to be some floozy that gets all naked for a silly magazine."

"*PlayDragon* is *not* a silly magazine," he said with his teeth slightly bared.

She just blinked impassively at him.

"Fine," he said, turning on his dragon cunning. "Leave then."

"Good."

"I'll just find someone else to be the first woman to be photographed for the soon-to-be largest publication to fine gentlemen in all of the Underworld."

"Good. You do that." Tazdoreena turned the handle and then paused. "The what?"

"Yes," Winchester said, sauntering away. "Ononokin will have another famous lady, known from one end of the continent to the other. It need not be you."

He gestured for her to leave.

"Please don't let me stand in the way of your career as a...what was it again?"

"Dental assistant," she muttered.

"Yes, that's right. A dental assistant." (For all their faults, orcs, ogres, and trolls had some of the nicest sets of pearly whites in all of Ononokin.) "That *does* sound far more appealing than having every wealthy suitor in the land knocking at your door," Winchester said sarcastically.

"I still get the two gold we agreed upon?"

"For leaving? I should say not."

"No," Tazdoreena said, stripping down. "I'm not leaving, lizard. I'm going to be famous. Now get the fans rolling and let's do this."

"Well," Winchester replied, "if you insist."

# THE NEW ADDITION

*T*he council room was a wreck.

The archery class had finished minutes before the wizards took over the room. The students never bothered to pick up after themselves, so arrows and throwing knives littered the floor and a spattering of dust hung in the air. It was all Treneth could do to keep from sneezing.

As soon as he was named chair of this wretched guild, things would change. He would either have this place kept tidy or he would find a new auditorium. His target was an organization worthy of true wizards, assuming he could find any.

"...and so," Muppy was saying as if eating a lemon, "it is my recommendation that Treneth of Dahl be added as a full-time member of the council."

Zotrinder's jaw was slack and Ibork was, for the first time that Treneth had ever witnessed, at a loss for words.

"Huh?" the Croomplatt twins chimed, making a slight departure from their normal response.

Treneth had fully expected this reaction. It was no secret

that he was disliked. He was a man of action. Wizards preferred inaction, as a general rule. He was confident that the motion would get passed, though. After all, Muppy's reputation was at stake.

"Who has been managing the legal house for the last five years?" she said with a twitch. Nobody answered. "How many of you have participated in the scholastic programs at Blitlaray's Magic Academy?"

Treneth watched their faces. They all avoided looking at each other and none would look at him or the chairperson. Muppy was doing well so far.

"I think it's clear that Treneth of Dahl has earned a seat amongst his...peers."

"Ha." The chorus was well subdued.

"Unless there are any objections, and unless there is a volunteer for the plethora of jobs that he handles, I move for the acceptance of Treneth of Dahl as full member of the council."

There were no objections. There were no acceptances either, but that wasn't a requirement of guild process.

Treneth found that he was the only one smiling. *So be it*, he thought.

He adopted a more professional look and moved to the front wall where Muppy stood.

"Treneth of Dahl," she said, looking more through him than at him, "do you swear to abide by the rules of the council?"

"I do."

"He'll be the first."

"Shut up, Ibork," Zotrinder said.

"Ha."

Muppy cleared her throat. "Will you continue to oversee the legal house duties and see to the academy's needs?"

Treneth wanted to rebuke the requirement. It was not an

enforceable rule. Clearly none of the other members were subject to such tidings. But, considering it gave him more control, he saw no harm in it.

"I will," he replied smoothly.

"Then we accept you as a member of the council of the Wizards' Guild, effective on this day. May whichever of The Twelve you believe in, if any, watch over any decisions you make on behalf of wizards in this land."

Treneth stood and adjusted his lapel.

"I just want to say that—"

"No speeches today," said Muppy, cutting him off. "You may have the seat next to Councilman Zotrinder."

"Why me?" Zotrinder said.

Treneth took a deep breath and calmed himself. Then he circled around to his seat. He sighed as Zotrinder leaned as far away as possible to the opposite side of his chair.

Only one more step to go and Treneth would be the leader of this guild.

Muppy had proven that she was not a worthy opponent. She would be on guard from this point on, for certain, but one day she would slip up or get lax. On that day, Treneth would make his move.

*In due time*, he told himself.

Vigilance *and* patience.

# MUGGING A WIZARD?

*W*imat Station was classy compared to Aopow. Travelers flowed in from Xarpney and Dakmenhem in the Underworld, two of the wealthier lands, so special attention was made on keeping the station clean and accessible.

Shops and restaurants covered the three-story complex. Sales signs, discounts, and a plethora of special offers littered the windows. Anything one could imagine, one could get at this plaza, even if it meant having to order it through Xarpney.

One of the nicest bits for Whizzfiddle was that the electromagnetic field was kept in check. This made magic allowable. Station security was clear that it should only be used in self-defense, and they had placed sensors throughout the complex. After what had happened in Aopow it was good to have his power accessible.

Whizzfiddle marched to an information booth and snatched a map before heading toward the eatery.

"I'm assuming you've each got enough left in your pockets to furnish yourselves with food?"

He didn't bother to await a response. Instead, he found a table near the back corner of the room and began running his finger across the connecting lines to the station. They had to get to Dakmenhem to pick up Winchester, and then he would jump them over to Civen Station. That would give a direct link into Kek. It would have been easier had Gungren not put them on the detour to Gorgan, but the past was the past. This new route would have to do.

He spotted Zel and Orophin ordering at one of the fast food establishments, McKorgnal's. Bekner and Gungren were milling about in front of Bugner Queen. They looked confused.

Whizzfiddle sighed.

He was certain they could all read. The issue was that in order to compete with the classier restaurants on Wimat, the fast food joints used menu names that were confusing to the working class. "Chicken de Sorteni" and "Beef Froopahn" were Whizzfiddle's personal favorites. These were better known as chicken on a stick and beef on a bun, respectively.

He turned his attention back to the map, when a shadow approached.

"You Whizzfiddle?" a voice asked.

Whizzfiddle held up a finger to signify he needed a moment.

"So that's how it's going to be, is it?" the voice said and a chair was kicked over.

Whizzfiddle looked at his finger. Wrong one again.

"Looks like we got a tough guy, fellas."

"No, no," Whizzfiddle said, tucking the map away casually, "just a simple misunderstanding." He closed up his backpack. "What can I do for you, gentlemen?"

The one with the eyepatch moved in close. "Why don't you come with us so's we can show you?"

Whizzfiddle smiled and reached into his robe to pull

forth his flask.

"Uh-uh," Eyepatch said, taking the bottle from Whizzfiddle. "We know about you, wizard."

"Well," Whizzfiddle replied, "it seems you have me at a disadvantage, sir."

"Oh, that we do," Eyepatch said. "Eh, boys?"

The ruffians chuckled.

Whizzfiddle scratched his beard for a moment. "It seems we have a bit of a dilemma, gentlemen."

"I don't see no problem," replied Eyepatch.

"No? I shall help you spot it, then. It's basic mathematics, really. An issue of numbers. You see, there are only four of you while there are five of us. On top of that, one of mine is capable of throwing you fully across the room, which makes him a multiplier of sorts."

"Look at me shaking, wizard," Eyepatch said with a sneer.

Bekner cleared his throat.

Each of the villains looked back and then up, and then up a little more. Seeing the full size of Bekner would be convincing to most anyone to be on his best behavior.

"Now," Whizzfiddle said, plucking his flask back from Eyepatch, "we were muscled out of Aopow Station because we weren't prepared." He took a deep pull and felt the power fill his veins. He thought it may be a good idea to have the power flowing for the rest of this little adventure, just in case. "But," he continued, "now we're tired and hungry and a little fed up with the run of bad luck we've been having. I'd have to say that a little knocking of heads might be exactly the thing we need to bring us back to life. What do you think, Zel?"

Zel was trembling and there seemed to be the beginnings of a damp area at the base of his trousers, but he stood tall.

"I fe...feel very unhappy right n...now," Zel answered.

"Well, look at that." Whizzfiddle rested his hand on

Eyepatch's shoulder. "I believe you've got our knight so angry that he can barely talk."

"Not worried about the knight," Eyepatch said.

Orophin moved over to Zel and stood a bit in front of him. "I'll keep him at bay," he said. "I wouldn't want the knight to do anything rash before I have my fun with you boys."

Bekner, Zel, Gungren, and Whizzfiddle raised their eyebrows.

"Not worried about the elf either," Eyepatch said. Then he seemed to think better of it. "Okay, I'm a little worried about what his idea of *fun* is."

Whizzfiddle noted that all of the assailants had eyes firmly set on Bekner. Understandable since the largest of the four barely crested the dwarf's chest. Plus, everyone knew the heart of a dwarf.

"I see you're worried about the wrong one," Whizzfiddle said jovially. "He can't throw you across the room. Well, maybe he could, but I would be more concerned over my smaller comrade, if I were you."

Just then, Gungren grabbed one of the men by his jacket and lifted him cleanly off the floor. The man grunted a curse. Gungren threw him over a few tables and then sank an elbow into the next thug's stomach, doubling him over and bringing him face to face with the dinky giant.

"Hello," Gungren said and then head-butted him.

Eyepatch tried to squirm away, but Bekner snaked out a hand and grabbed him by the noggin, lifted him up, and punched him squarely in the nose. More accurately, the punch was aimed at Eyepatch's nose but encompassed his entire face.

The last roughneck took a swing at Orophin. The elf ducked and the punch caught the comatose Zel, knocking him from his feet. Orophin snapped a perfectly timed fist to the attacker's groin area, causing the man to shriek and double over.

Whizzfiddle shouted a spell.

Time seemed to stand still as blue light shot from the tip of his wand, engulfing all of the bad guys, even pulling the one Gungren had thrown back. They writhed and groaned as the magic twisted them in a tornado-like fury. After he felt that they had had enough, he released them and they crashed to the floor, unconscious.

"We should be going," Whizzfiddle said after a few moments. "Station Watch will be here any minute."

"Already here," a man in a bright red uniform said. "You do know that destructive magic is not allowed in Wimat Station?"

"I know that it is allowable as a means of defense, sir. And if you'd be so kind as to look around you, you'll see that I was in need of defense."

The officer looked about, taking in the five bodies on the ground. He motioned his men to action and then each grabbed a man and started cuffing them.

"No, wait," Orophin said, taking Zel away from one of the officers. "He's with us. They, uh, caught him by surprise."

"Take 'em away, boys," the officer said. "I'll catch up to you in a minute." He turned his attention to Whizzfiddle. "Listen, wizard, from the looks of your own goons I don't think you needed to use that magic. I have a mind to haul you down to the station for re-education." Bekner turned and gazed down at the man. "However," the officer squeaked, clearly remembering that he'd just told his men to leave the scene, "seeing as that it was in self-defense and all, I'll let it slide this time."

"Very kind of you, sir," Whizzfiddle said. "Once we finish our meals we'll be on our way and out of your jurisdiction."

"Yes," the officer said, backing away. "Yes, you do that."

## A MAGAZINE AT WORK

*F*ilming crawled on as Winchester did all he could to work Tazdoreena into a sensual rage.

The camera just didn't love her.

They'd tried multiple outfits, fans, lighting effects, and Blerg even stood in a few of the pictures. He was fully clothed and trying to look like a bouncer at a club. It was to give that dancer-being-protected visage. It failed, mostly, but with his budget and time-to-market requirement, Winchester forced himself to be satisfied.

Three hours of snapping was all he could do before calling a halt to the shoot.

"That's a wrap," Winchester said. "We should have enough to go on. With luck we can pull some decent shots for the spread. Oknot, take these rolls to development and put a rush on it. Thank you, Tazdoreena," he added and then slunk off to his office.

It would be a couple more hours before he got a peek at the photos, so he gave another look at the layout.

The page was not as clean and crisp as his miniaturized dragon-brain wanted. He was a visionary, not a designer.

Maybe after the first issue was put out he would be able to hire someone with a better eye for design.

He leaned back and placed his hands behind his head. What he needed was a little time with one of his own. Not a lizard, but a dragon. A large female beast that he could ravish with his critical eye. Preferably mature so that she would be properly experienced.

"Mr. Hargrath?"

Winchester opened his eyes and saw Qayla standing at his door. He thought certain she had used his name, and did she really say "mister?"

"Yes, Qayla?"

She looked at her feet. "I want maybe you photo me for book."

Oh boy.

"Oh?"

"Heard about famous thing."

Winchester sat dumbfounded. She was a sweet woman, for an ogre. But, alas, she was an ogre.

He would have to turn on that dragon charm and dissuade her somehow.

"Come take a look at the layout, Qayla," he said, motioning her in. "What do you think?"

"Cemetery off."

"What? Oh! Symmetry." He smiled and then looked back at the page. "Is it?"

"Yep," she said and then grabbed at his markers and started drawing on the page. "Put line here and color thing here."

Winchester gasped as the page came to life. With just the couple of tweaks Qayla had done, she had already improved the layout tenfold.

"Qayla," he said, staring at the page, "I can't believe it. You've an eye for design!"

"I do?"

"Oh yes," Winchester affirmed, staring at the page. "I've got a better job for you than modeling."

"You do?"

"I do, my dear," he said, "I do indeed!"

He was rubbing his hands together as Blerg walked in.

"One moment, Blerg," Winchester said. "Qayla, pull up a chair and go through this entire layout. Make any adjustments you think will fit best and we'll have a magazine that will shine."

"So, you need me to make it look good?"

"Yes, yes. Oh, yes."

"I be model in book?"

"Hmmm? Oh, that." He cleared his throat. "It's just that, you see, well, there is a—"

She gently placed the marker back on the table. "If I no model, I no do design."

"But Qayla, you'd be listed as the designer of the publication." Hers was a visage of confusion. "I mean *book*," Winchester corrected. "You'll be listed as the designer of the book."

She nodded.

"Your name will be shown in the credits and everything. There will be magazine offers for your design skills. You'll have money and fame."

She seemed thoughtful. It was hard to tell with an ogre, though. It could have been gas.

After a few moments, her eyes uncrossed.

"No," she said softly. "Both or none."

The layout of the magazine was centered around the photos of one lady. It would take a lot of work to redo the pages to support more than one model. Worse yet, where Tazdoreena was barely passable, Qayla was not passable at all.

Still, he had to think of the success of the magazine over all else, even if that meant sacrificing design.

"My equal that pays me," Blerg said, "we talk now."

"Sure, Blerg, sure," Winchester said, waving. "In a few minutes."

"No," he said, "now. Qayla, out a minute." Blerg didn't wait for a response. He shuffled Qayla out of the room and then turned the lock on the door.

"What's the meaning of this, Blerg?"

"You vision need bigger."

"I'm not sure what you mean."

"You think orc all sexy and none else," Blerg said.

"Dragons, too, of course."

"What?"

"I think orcs *and* dragons are sexy," Winchester said. "Not just orcs."

"Yeah, well, ogre and troll sexy to some and there more ogre and troll than orc and dragon. Even vampire and werewolf sexy to some…can't say why though."

"I don't follow you, Blerg."

"Market bigger than orc and dragon. You need think bigger."

How could bringing non-orcs and non-dragons in make for better marketing?

He opened his mouth to retort and then stopped.

Of course!

Why hadn't he seen this before? Because he was a dragon, that's why.

Dragons *all* thought that orcs and dragons were attractive, but the other races, particularly humans, were an abomination to the visual plain. For the sake of *PlayDragon*, Winchester had no choice but to accept that a larger demographic meant higher returns.

Between Qayla and Blerg, Winchester had just found a

new respect for ogres.

"Blerg," Winchester said, astonished, "you're a genius."

Blerg appeared aware of this fact. He unlatched the door and called Qayla back in.

"Qayla," Winchester said, "it'll take a number of hours and a lot of hard work, but I need you to redo the entire layout of *PlayDragon*. We're going to have multiple models, including you!"

"We is?"

"You can thank our good friend, Blerg."

Qayla edged up next to Blerg. "I not know what you say, but I like that you say it."

"What go on in here?" Patty said as she burst into the room, looking intently at Qayla and Blerg. "I tell you, Qayla, before about funny stuff and having self-steamer!"

"Patty," Winchester said, "it's all fine. Qayla is going to work on the layout of *PlayDragon*. She has quite an eye for arrangement."

"And?" Qayla and Blerg said together.

"Oh, right, and she's also going to be one of the models in the publication. Erm, I mean book."

Patty looked flabbergasted. "You is?"

Qayla nodded.

"But what about self-steamer?"

"Patty," Winchester said, "Qayla has self-stea...self-esteem. She is proud of her body. She has confidence."

"That right," Qayla said, drawing herself up.

"But men look at pictures, with no good thought."

"Some will admire the artistic beauty of the nude female," Winchester attempted.

Patty smirked and waggled a finger at Winchester. "More like horny man look at naughty nudey."

"Well—"

"She right," Qayla said, stopping Winchester. "But I okay

with it. I like idea of man being stupid and me have power on him."

"Power?" they all replied.

"Man think he have power, yeah? But when woman sexy on him his brain not work same." She ran a hand across Blerg's face. He turned a nice shade of green, which was the color ogres subscribed to for blushing. The poor oaf took on an expression of a dullard. "See?"

Winchester did. He had seen the effect a number of times on friends and contacts. While he loved the ladies, likely more than any healthy male should, he was never affected in this way by them. In fact, it was the fairer sex who tended to melt in his presence.

Oknot walked past the door and looked inside.

"There you is," he said as he walked up to Patty. "I look every place. You not clean up set like you say you was gonna. This place got to be clean, yeah? How that happen if you not do your work?"

Patty reached up and touched Oknot's face. His coloring changed and his eyes went glassy.

"You clean set for me while I talk here?"

After a few blinks, Oknot nodded dumbly and walked back out.

"See what I say?" Qayla said, smiling.

Everyone stood silently for a few moments.

Qayla had just put the company's mission statement together, even if she didn't know it.

**PlayDragon**, *where women use their sexy to take the man's brain away.*

"I model too," Patty said suddenly.

"No, no, no," Winchester replied. "We barely have time to get things going with two models."

Patty took two steps and put her hand on Winchester's face. He rolled his eyes at her. She looked confused.

"It's not magic, Patty," he said. "Not every male you touch is going to fall into some mental stupor."

Patty looked down at him and furrowed her brow menacingly. She slammed her hands onto Winchester's desk and brought her face within inches of his, her eyes threatening to set him aflame.

"I model too," she growled.

"As you wish," he replied, feeling his brain switch off.

## STANDING UP, FALLING DOWN

*R*impertuz strolled in a few minutes late. Treneth lifted an eyebrow, but his apprentice withheld his apology.

"You realize you're late?"

"Yes, sir."

Treneth's other eyebrow joined the first. "Have you nothing to say?"

"Nothing that I can think of," Rimpertuz replied, and then added, "sir."

"Must we go through yet another round—"

"Sir," Rimpertuz interrupted, "I don't mind that I am treated somewhat poorly at times; I am an apprentice. But what we did against the council chair was wrong, in my estimation."

"Is that so?"

"Yes, sir."

"Well, well, Rimpertuz," Treneth said, leaning back in his chair, "I do believe you are smitten with our dear Muppy."

Rimpertuz turned a shade of red and his eyes creased. "*My* dear Muppy."

It was the first time Treneth had ever seen Rimpertuz's temper rise, and he did not find it appealing in the least.

"Remember your place, *my* apprentice," he said icily. "I could have you removed from the apprenticeship program and placed onto the next transport back to Kespers with a snap of my fingers."

"Do it, then," Rimpertuz said.

Treneth hesitated.

"That's what I thought." Rimpertuz strolled over and sat down, stepping firmly on the creaky floorboard. "The bottom line is that I know what you did and therefore I can clear Muppy's name and have you charged with conspiracy."

Treneth nodded slowly. He wasn't sure whether to feel pride or pity for his apprentice. On the one hand, the man was showing some resolve and creativity; on the other hand, he was stepping into a form of independence that would make for an unpleasant master-student relationship.

"I applaud you, Rimpertuz," Treneth said after some time. "You are showing the shrewdness that I have tried to feed you over these years."

Rimpertuz sat up a little taller, and Treneth leaned forward, placing his elbows on the desk.

"Alas, you have still had relations with the council chair. So while you could bring evidence against me for having arranged the initial meeting, you would also be indicting yourself and *your* dear Muppy."

Rimpertuz slouched again.

After a few moments, Rimpertuz stood up and pushed the chair back to its original position. He walked back to the door, avoiding the creaky floorboard, placed his hands behind his back, and took on his normal demeanor.

"I apologize for being late, sir."

Treneth grinned.

"Think nothing of it."

# THE HOTEL

*D*akmenhem hadn't changed much since the last time Whizzfiddle had been there.

It was a city that sat near the coast and was quite near sea level. The cobblestone streets were filthy and the air was heavy with a dank and fishy odor. It flooded often during the rainy seasons. The city engineers had built dams and drainage systems that helped contain the worst of it, but there was only so much that could be pumped out when the waves came in.

"What are those buildings?" Bekner asked.

"They're hotels," Whizzfiddle answered. "Same as in the Upperworld, just a lot taller."

"What about those posts with the ropes connecting them?"

"Those are TalkyThingy lines. People here are able to have conversations with each other without being in the same room."

"We do that in Restain," Gungren said. "It called yelling."

That was an understatement. The last time Whizzfiddle had been in Restain he nearly had gone deaf. He had sworn never again to enter the land of the giants without a pair of earmuffs.

"Gentlemen, there are a number of things you will see that are strange to you. Some things may seem familiar. This is because people from here often visit us as we are now visiting them."

"Vampires," said Orophin as he pointed at a couple of men having a conversation by a street lamp.

The men were wearing black capes and had slicked-back hair. Their skin was white and pasty, much like Zel's appearance at the moment.

Whizzfiddle pushed Orophin's hand down.

"It's not nice to point," he said. "Yes, those are vampires. There are also orcs, trolls, ogres, werewolves, and various other species that you have been told of in your legends."

"Are you after saying the legends are all real?" Bekner asked quietly.

"I hope so," Orophin said, keeping his gaze on the vampires.

"No," Whizzfiddle answered. "Many of them are not real at all." He waved his hand in front of Orophin. "Especially the one about vampires."

"There are vampires in the Upperworld too," Zel said. "I used to deport them all the time."

"There are?"

"Yes, Orophin, there are," answered Whizzfiddle. "Most of them are there illegally, so they are careful to avoid detection. You've come in contact with a number of them over the years, no doubt."

"I think I would have known if I'd come in contact—"

"Mosquitoes."

"Pardon?"

Everyone backed away.

"No," Orophin said, "not that. I mean why did you say mosquitoes?"

"That's what vampires turn into when they want to fly and feed."

"You mean bats."

"No, I don't mean bats."

Orophin looked horrified. "I've smacked hundreds of those things."

"They're quite resilient, I assure you."

"I like this place," Gungren said, interrupting the conversation. "It smell like home."

"Indeed," said Whizzfiddle and then he moved into the crowd and headed for the only hotel that was run by the trolls.

Hotel Gakoonk.

The trolls treated it like their hometown of Gakoonk. Though not particularly attractive creatures, trolls were excellent in the realm of hospitality. They were even better at charging for it.

The troll who served as doorman was more hideous than most. His nose alone was bulbous enough to use as a float on a fishing expedition. After looking over the troop, the troll pulled the door open and gestured them inside.

The place was posh. Checkered marble floors ran throughout the lobby. Expertly etched dark mahogany boards topped with decorative crown molding lined the walls. Even the furniture was trimmed in fine leather with gold beading.

"You've got no reservation?"

"Not exactly," Whizzfiddle said to the clerk. He then pulled forth his bag of gold. It was depleting quickly. He acted as if he'd accidentally dropped a piece on the other side of the reception desk. The clerk picked it up and looked at

Whizzfiddle questioningly. "It seems you've found a piece of gold there, my good man...I mean, *troll*."

Trolls hated to be referred to as men.

The troll snorted.

"So it does. Hmmm...wait a tick or two." He looked at a box of some sort. "I believe I have found your reservation after all, my dear troll." Trolls had no reservations calling men trolls. "It says here that the reservation is for four persons—"

"Five."

"—five persons. Staying for two—"

"One."

"—one night."

He clicked away on a pad that sat on the desk.

"What's that after being?" Bekner asked, pointing at the troll's keypad.

"Not now," Whizzfiddle said, hushing him.

"What was the question?" the troll asked.

"Nothing, my good troll," Whizzfiddle said. "One of our lot just needs to use the facilities. Erm, I mean he needs to use the can."

The troll nodded and pointed toward the restrooms.

"I'm sure it can wait until we're settled," Whizzfiddle said.

"Aye, it can at that," Bekner agreed.

"The room is ten gold for the night," the troll said.

"*Ten?*"

The troll turned the box toward Whizzfiddle. The amount glowed in jarring digital clarity.

"That's how much the top suite costs, my good troll," he said, showing his perfect smile. "It does encompass the entire floor, and will allow for any additional guests. And do note that if you need help finding any additional guests," the troll added with a wink, "we can assist you there as well."

"Right," Whizzfiddle said and handed over the coins.

# VISITING WINCHESTER

*P*hotographs were strewn all over the walls and desks. Tazdoreena, Qayla, and Patty were literally on display, and they looked fantastic, depending on whether you were a dragon, orc, or ogre. Trolls weren't being represented in this issue.

Winchester wore his little red velvet robe as he worked on narrowing the list of photos that would make the issue. His tail's throbbing was buried to the point of a dull ache as his excitement mounted. It had started with hundreds of snapshots and was now down to just over twenty each.

Qayla was working diligently on the layout. It was coming together better than Winchester had expected.

He still wasn't sold on Tazdoreena being his cover model, but there wasn't a lot of choice. She had been a little peeved that there were going to be other girls in the magazine, but Winchester had assured her that she would be no less popular for sharing the pages. She had just given him a dirty look and walked out.

He would keep his word, of course. Once a dragon gives his word, it was solid. One just had to be careful to understand precisely what the word was that a dragon had given.

"My equal that pays me," Blerg said, "there's some people here to see you."

Winchester raised his head from his work. People? He wasn't expecting to see any people.

So Curdles wasn't even going to give him a week? That was one of the bigger differences between dragons and orcs: orcs weren't known for keeping their word. To be fair, they weren't known for giving their word, either.

"Tell them I'm not here," Winchester said. "I'll sneak out the back and buy us some time."

"You want me to lie?"

"Blerg, if they throw me in that tank we'll never get this magazine done," he said frantically.

Blerg took in a deep breath and slowly let it out. The average ogre would sell his own grandmother for a popsicle. Blerg proved more and more each day that he was not your average ogre.

"You owe me one," he said and stormed out of the office.

Winchester threw off his robe and bolted for the back door, slipping through the doggy flap he'd had installed when they'd moved in. It was much simpler than asking someone to open it for him.

Just as he cleared the door he ran directly into the foot of Zooks.

"Going somewhere?" Curdles said, picking up Winchester by his still-aching tail.

"You said I had a week!"

Curdles shook his head. "Still stereotyping me with other orcs, lizard? You'll get your week, but I've decided that you need a little supervision. Yultza here is going to watch over the establishment a bit for me."

"That is just…" Then he paused. "Yultza?"

"Yeah," Curdles said. "That a problem?"

"No, no," Winchester said. "Actually, that would be quite helpful."

"Oh?"

"Yes. We could, um, use the muscle."

# YOU SCRATCH MY BACK

*T*reneth was going through the stack of legal documents that he'd brought home from the council meeting.

Of the twenty-seven wizard contracts that he had already processed, twenty-six of them had not been fulfilled to the letter. The twenty-seventh one hadn't been fulfilled at all. Had he so desired, Treneth resolved that he could make a living doing nothing but persecuting wizards for not upholding the guild rules.

His TalkyThingy started to jingle.

"Yeah," Treneth said, remembering how Teggins had answered earlier.

"They're in Dakmenhem," Teggins said.

"Who?"

"Your wizard friend, Treneth. Who do you think?"

"I thought you said they were in Gorgan?"

"They were and they should have been stuck there for at least a couple of weeks, but somehow they got out. My men ran into them at Wimat Station."

Treneth grabbed a map of the stations that Rimpertuz

had picked up a few weeks prior. The layout was confusing at best, but he spotted Wimat and saw that it connected to Kek. That Whizzfiddle was in Dakmenhem was a good sign. Being in the Underworld meant that he was still a good ways away from hooking up with Pecklesworthy.

"Why didn't they stop them?"

"According to my men," Teggins said, "the wizard had an entourage of bodyguards and the station police were in the area. There was nothing they could do."

"I don't want excuses, Teggins," Treneth said in a huff.

"Watch it, Treneth. You ain't exactly cleared my name with the council."

"As a matter of fact, I have. The papers are signed and filed. And I'll have you also know that I'm a full-fledged member of the council now."

There was silence.

"So," Treneth continued, "I will expect better action from you."

"You're saying that I'm all set up there?" Teggins said.

"That's what I said. Now, you just need to finish your end of the bargain."

"I'd say we're done," Teggins replied. "I delayed Whizzfiddle twice and I told you I couldn't kill him. Not much more I can do."

Treneth fumed. It was another case of putting his beliefs on others. He would complete his end of any bargain, but Teggins and most of the populace of Ononokin took a different view.

"One more thing, Treneth," Teggins said. "I would recommend that you not travel to my city for at least a couple of years, and I'll be sending you a little message soon so you'll know I'm serious."

"Is that a threat?"

"Absolutely."

"Oh." Nobody ever answered the "Is that a threat?" question directly. Usually, they responded with something clever, like, "I don't make threats" or "No, it's a promise." Sure, it meant the same thing, but it was just more ominous. "Save your threats," Treneth said, trying to gain the upper hand again. "Or I'll make a few of my own."

"Now you're talking my language," Teggins replied. "I like working with threats. It's most efficient."

"Good day, Teggins," Treneth said as he shut down the connection.

As long as Idoon's shipment arrived before Whizzfiddle did, things would continue moving smoothly on the plan to disbar his former master. At this point Treneth had no choice but to rely on Pecklesworthy being incapable of helping Whizzfiddle.

Treneth's vengeance wasn't as important as his position in the council but, again, he followed through with his obligations...even those he made with himself.

# THE WIZARD AND THE LOAN SHARK

*W*hizzfiddle and his troop were standing in the middle of a little office. There were desks, fans, cameras, lighting pods, and a bed that was tucked in the corner. The cameras were all facing the bed. He wasn't sure he wanted to know what kind of business this was.

An ogre, who had introduced himself as "Blerg," was explaining that Winchester was currently out on an appointment.

The back door opened and a gruff-looking orc walked in. He was holding a lizard upside down by its tail.

"Curdles?" Whizzfiddle said, thinking he recognized the orc.

"Whizzfiddle?" Curdles said back.

"Whizzfiddle?" the lizard said, and then looked past him. "Orophin? Bekner? Gungren? Zel?"

They all stood across from each other. Nobody moved, except Winchester—who was wriggling a bit.

"Could you please let me down? Ahhhh—ouch," Winchester said as he hit the floor.

Whizzfiddle adjusted his hat as he eyed Curdles, who was

177

adjusting his tie. It was a little odd to see an orc in a suit, but Whizzfiddle had to admit that the pinstriped look had always worked for the mob boss.

"What are you doin' in my town?" Curdles asked.

"Your town?" Winchester said, eyebrows raised.

"Figure of speech."

"I take it you guys know each other?" Orophin said.

Whizzfiddle muttered a "hmmm" and then grabbed his flask. He took a quick swig as Curdles smiled at him.

"You know your magic ain't gonna be fast enough for Zooks's bullets," he said, grinning.

"You misunderstand, Curdles," Whizzfiddle said. "I believe the last time we parted it was my turn to buy the rounds. I'm not powering up, I'm numbing up."

Everyone stood their distance, mumbling in confusion.

Whizzfiddle finally couldn't stay in character any further and began to giggle. Curdles burst out into a full laugh and they crossed the chasm and shook hands.

"I guess that answers that," Orophin said.

## LET'S HAVE DRINKS

*S*will was a kind description for the ale in Curdles's favorite tavern, Benpo's. It was a shade of greenish-brown that smelled like it looked, and tasted worse. Even if you could stomach the brew, the mental ramifications would likely set your soul aflame. It had won the "Worst Ale in Dakmenhem" award the last seven years in a row. Fortunately, Whizzfiddle had already suffered the wrath of Benpo's brew once before. He put a protection spell on himself to counteract the slurried liquid.

The pub itself was pleasant enough. Whizzfiddle especially enjoyed the billiard tables. They were handcrafted by the finest artisans, stained in different hues, and stretched with multiple felt styles. He had once considered making room in his house to have one of his own, but the transportation costs were outrageous and he was awful at the game anyway.

Orophin, however, appeared to be quite adept with the stick and balls. The elf had been winning all night. It could have been his skill or it could have been that his entourage consisted of a knight, a little giant, and a gigantic dwarf.

"I can't say that it's good to see you, Zooks," Whizzfiddle said to Curdles's henchman.

"Likewise."

"Ha!" Whizzfiddle said with a wink. "You haven't changed a bit. Just as surly as ever."

"You look the same too, wizard."

"I would," Whizzfiddle said with a sigh. "Long-life elixir and all, if you remember."

Zooks grunted and resumed his drinking. He never was one for conversation.

"Yultza is new to your team, Curdles," Whizzfiddle said. "I thought you didn't believe in diversification?"

"She surprised me," Curdles said. "I don't surprise easily. And don't let her looks fool ya. She's capable."

Whizzfiddle didn't have enough booze in his veins to consider an orc's "looks." Winchester definitely seemed taken by her, though. He had been sitting next to her and chatting her up ever since they'd sat down.

"So why are you here, old man?"

Whizzfiddle pointed at the lizard. "For him."

"Is that right?"

"Sadly, yes. It seems that he was part of a troop caught in one of Pecklesworthy's transfigurations."

"Group spell," Curdles said.

"Indeed. And you know how it is with those."

"All or nothing."

Whizzfiddle leaned forward and whispered, "I take it you have designs on him as well?"

"He owes me money."

Whizzfiddle nodded and took a pull from the mug. It took some effort to swallow. There was nothing quite like a nice, lumpy ale.

"How much?"

"Now, you know that's—"

"One hundred and fifty gold," Zooks said, and then looked at Curdles. "Oh, sorry, boss."

"I can cover that," Whizzfiddle said. "I'll just need to stop off at the bank."

Winchester stopped talking to Yultza.

"Really?" Winchester said.

"It's not free, Winchester," Whizzfiddle said. "And your reputation for trickery is legendary, so you may as well just hush up now."

"There's a bit of a problem that's come up," Curdles said, knocking on the table. "See, I've been thinking that instead of this being a straight-out loan, that it may instead be an investment. Diversification, if you will."

"Wise," Whizzfiddle said, tucking his purse away. There was no point in trying to pay off a mob boss looking to invest.

"Wait a second," Winchester said, stomping to the middle of the table. "We agreed on it being a loan, and I'll—"

"Shut up, lizard," Curdles said. "You ain't in a position of power here."

Winchester pointed, began to talk, shut his mouth, and then crossed his arms and looked away. He was much less threatening as a lizard than as a dragon.

"The way I see it," Curdles said, "you'll be cutting me in for twenty-five percent of all profits."

Winchester uncrossed his arms.

"So—"

"Don't worry, Winchester. I don't want to run the thing. I don't have an eye for it, and since you'll be photographing ogres and dragons, I don't have the stomach for it either."

"What about the aquarium?"

"If this *PlayDragon* thing of yours takes off, I'll buy me a lizard that don't speak."

"Done," Winchester said, "but…I need one more thing."

"Go on."

"Yultza."

"What?" Yultza and Curdles said in unison, followed a split-second later by Zooks.

"She is the perfect orc for the cover. She'll push this mag through the roof."

"No," she said.

"Wait." Curdles held up a finger. Whizzfiddle checked it— it was the correct one. "So," Curdles continued, "you're saying that if she poses nude in your magazine, that we'll see more money?"

"Easily double. Probably triple."

"No."

"Yultza," Curdles said, "you'll do it if I say you'll do it. Don't forget that you work for me, not the other way around."

She got up. "Not anymore."

"But...you'll be famous," Winchester said. "You'll be the first!"

"What will being famous do for me?"

"Well, you'll be rich, for one," Winchester said. "Plus, you'll have no need for a boss anymore."

"Hey now."

"Curdles," Winchester said seriously, "what's more important, ten percent of a highly successful magazine or one employee who leaves your service? And remember that it's good for her too, and she's the one who's going to be the cause of much more toward that five percent you're getting."

"Hmmm. Okay, you win this one. And it's twenty-five percent, lizard. Don't forget it."

Whizzfiddle shook his head and smiled. Dragons were cunning. Specifically *this* sagacious dragon. Demons were less shrewd than Winchester Hargrath Jr. III.

"Okay, I'll do it," Yultza said, "but I want one hundred gold to do it."

"One hundred!"

"Plus a percentage of any issue I'm in," she stated evenly.

They sat dumbfounded.

"It's either that or I walk."

"Done," Winchester said.

"Done?" Curdles said to Winchester. "What do you mean done? Where are you going to get a hundred gold, lizard?"

"You said it yourself, Curdles," Winchester replied, "I'm the one with the eye for this magazine. That makes you the one with the money."

"You should know better than to tangle with a dragon." Whizzfiddle laughed and then winced through another swallow of the ale.

"*Lizard*," Curdles muttered the correction.

"Sadly, there is still the problem of my group quest," Whizzfiddle said. "While I really hate to put your plans in jeopardy, Winchester is going to have to come with me."

# THE COUNCIL HAS CONCERNS

*I*bork and Zotrinder were waiting for Muppy when she arrived at the office. They had asked to see her, which was an odd occurrence for the weekend, made stranger by the fact that Zotrinder and Ibork despised one another.

They said their hellos as she plopped into her chair.

"This is about Treneth," she stated.

"What were you thinking?" Ibork blurted out.

"Yes," Zotrinder said. "I would seek your logic here as well."

She had been thinking over the last two days how best to answer this question. They would find out eventually, of course, but by the time they did she would have new twists and turns in place to cover herself. It was Wizarding-101.

Unfortunately, she had fallen a bit for Rimpertuz. He was young and vivacious, and he was smitten with her. She didn't want to spend the rest of her days covering things up. Why should she have to hide her relationship from the council, burying it from regulatory control? It was a stupid rule that was put in place simply for Treneth to use as leverage for his ploy.

It was time to come clean and change the record books.

"I did it to avoid a scandal."

"Scandal?" Zotrinder said as he paused from filing his nails.

"That's right," Muppy answered. "I have been in a relationship with Rimpertuz."

"What?"

"Treneth's apprentice?"

She leaned forward and looked over her clasped fingers.

"Gentlemen, we are all adults here. I know that the rules state that we are disallowed from having a relationship with an apprentice."

"Very clearly," Ibork said.

"However," Muppy continued, "it's an antiquated rule that needs to be removed from the books."

"It was just added a few meetings ago!"

"No, Ibork, it wasn't." Muppy opened the book and turned the page toward the halfling. "As you can see, the original rule is about a thousand years old. Lore says that it was written because Blitlaray's first apprentice had designs on him that he didn't share."

"Didn't we hold a vote on this rule recently?" Zotrinder said.

"Yes, we added verbiage that said a wizard-apprentice relationship was disallowed even if the apprentice was not studying under the wizard they were relating to, in a manner of speaking. And that's how our Treneth of Dahl worked to set me up."

"How so?"

She explained the events that led to the election of Treneth to the council.

"As you can see," she said, "it was either I get him appointed to the council or I fall into a scandal."

Zotrinder was grinning a little as Ibork's jaw hung open.

Muppy could pit the two men against each other. It wouldn't be the first time. But knowing them both, it was only a matter of time before their combined front fell to pieces.

"This is outrageous," Ibork said, his face reddening.

"Truly," Zontrinder responded, keeping his smirk. "Truly outrageous."

"You realize that you have single-handedly—"

"What exactly have I done, Ibork?"

"You let Treneth of Dahl get on the council!"

Zotrinder was giggling.

Muppy huffed. "We all knew that he was going to make it to council eventually. He's too devious not to. I think it's more likely that we're all just a tad bit jealous of just how clever our young Treneth can be."

"Dangerous," Ibork said, along with a jettison of spittle.

"And you're not, Ibork?" Zotrinder said. "And I'm not? Name a wizard who isn't dangerous."

"Whizzfiddle."

"Fair enough," Zotrinder conceded. "Neither is he all that manipulative. Never was, from what I recall."

"No," Muppy said, "but he's clearly smarter than we are. He *did* have the sense to dump Treneth from his apprenticeship."

"True," Zotrinder said.

As Muppy was trying to dig up dirt on Treneth, of which she found none, she came across the copy of Whizzfiddle's cessation letter. It had simply read, "The boy is too much of a stickler and I'm too old to stickle."

"Look," Muppy said. "Treneth's on the council. We can

bicker and fight all we want, but if we don't represent a combined front then he'll soon own this council."

"Outrageous!"

"You've already used that one, Ibork."

"Shut up, Zotrinder."

## A DONE DEAL

*T*he deal was done.

Winchester was going to go along and fulfill his return to being a dragon so that Whizzfiddle could satisfy the guild contract.

In turn, Whizzfiddle agreed to become the first subscriber to Winchester's upcoming publication. While the elderly wizard found little interest in naked orcs and dragons, he figured that five gold was a small price to pay in getting Winchester on board with the quest.

Winchester also insisted on making a stop-over in Xarpney before going to Kek. This detour worried Whizzfiddle a bit, but one rarely got the solid end of a deal when negotiating with dragons.

Blerg was going to run the day-to-day operations of *PlayDragon* with a little help from Zooks and a lot of oversight from Curdles.

Yultza had insisted on journeying with Winchester to make sure that he came back.

And for all this, Whizzfiddle promised to keep Winchester and Yultza safe. Plus two hundred gold to

Curdles and a round of ale the next ten times he was in town. Curdles always came out ahead.

"Lads," Whizzfiddle said as he exited the pub with the troop, "let's head back to the hotel and get ourselves a decent night of sleep. Tomorrow we're off to Kek to get everything squared away."

"Xarpney first," Winchester reminded him.

"Briefly."

It was only a few blocks to the hotel, which gave Whizzfiddle enough time to think. He would give them all a quick reminder on the importance of tenacity, focusing mostly on Winchester and Gungren. They were edging closer to completing this little quest and he needed it to end right.

"Now, remember," Whizzfiddle said to them as they entered the lobby, "the more you embrace what you have become, the harder it's going to be for Pecklesworthy to undo it."

"Don't you think it's going to be a little too late?" Winchester said. "It's not like we're a week into this, wizard."

"Yes," Whizzfiddle said, looking from face to face, "I do know."

"Good."

"Look, Winchester," Whizzfiddle said, "you were at the battle with these people when they were normal."

"Normal is a relative term."

"Nevertheless," Whizzfiddle continued, "they all want to be back to their old selves."

"I don't," Gungren said.

"Nor I," Winchester agreed. "I've grown rather fond of my new perspective."

"Which is exactly my point. You are the two who are jeopardizing the success of these three returning to what they were. The only thing you're going to miss is a week or two of Dakmenhem. Then you get to come back, resume your work, and have the knowledge that you've allowed these others to get on with their lives."

"Yeah, yeah," Winchester said. "I agreed already, didn't I?"

"As long as you fully understand what you agreed to," Whizzfiddle replied.

"How come he get go back?" Gungren asked.

Whizzfiddle grunted. He'd had a feeling this was going to come up. Why couldn't Pecklesworthy have just made the giant little and be done with it? Why make him smart too?

"It was in our agreement," Whizzfiddle said.

"I want go back too."

"Now, Gungren—"

"No, now," Gungren said, squaring his shoulders. "Lizard go back, so does I."

Whizzfiddle closed his eyes and pinched the top of his nose. His head ached from all this work, and probably a bit from Benpo's ale. There was enough juice in his veins to allow a small incantation to clear things up.

"*And* I want be your 'prentice."

"Oh no," Whizzfiddle answered as they headed upstairs, "not going to happen."

"Then I not doing it."

"I'm not having this discussion, Gungren. You signed a contract with the Wizards' Guild. If you don't fulfill that contract, you will never get your license to be a wizard anyway. It's one of those rock-and-a-hard-place situations, you see?"

Gungren frowned and crossed his arms, stomping harder than he had to as they approached the gate at the top floor.

Whizzfiddle pushed at the gate, but it wouldn't open.

"Hmmm," he said, rubbing his chin. "Maybe I have to say something to open it?"

He cleared his throat.

"Open presto," he declared.

Gungren groaned. "It 'open sesame' or 'presto,' not both. You may be great wizard but you no good for street magic."

"Are you sure? I thought certain it was 'open presto.'"

"It not. Look, you got use the card thing."

Gungren reached into Whizzfiddle's pocket and pulled a couple of cards out. He placed one of the cards into the slot at the top of the stairs and the gate opened.

"Presto," he said sarcastically.

They entered the floor and found a large room with doors on all sides. The suite was luxurious indeed, and the entire floor was theirs. At ten gold a night it was a ripoff, but it would do nicely in helping Whizzfiddle to keep everyone in check.

"Now," Whizzfiddle said, motioning them all to pick a room, "I want each of you to go to sleep. I trust you all understand the gravity of our quest at this point and will act responsibly until we complete it."

They all stared at him.

"Well?" Whizzfiddle said, jarring them to action. "We leave early in the morning."

Gungren dropped the access cards on the table in the middle of the room, mumbled something about Whizzfiddle not being fair, and then walked to the last door.

One by one, the rest disappeared into various rooms. Winchester shared his room with Yultza.

Whizzfiddle walked to the opposite side and entered the master suite. Ostentatious was the only word to describe it. Gold linens, an enormous soaking tub, and a view of Dakmenhem that was fit for a king.

This was no time for pleasantries, though. At some point he would come back to vacation here, but for now he was tired. He refilled his flask, took a couple of sips, and topped it off again.

Looking out the window, Whizzfiddle could see the life of Dakmenhem. It was a party town. There were clubs, pubs, games, rides, street magic, and...

"Oh, damn," he said as he bolted back into the main hallway.

He rapped on each door.

Orophin opened.

Zel opened.

Bekner opened.

Winchester's room was empty and so was Gungren's.

Whizzfiddle flopped down on the leather couch and rubbed his eyes. He should have known better than to trust them. They were too much like him.

He pressed a button on the table beside him and the curtains opened to reveal a vast skyline. The others sat down and joined him in looking outside. It was quite a sight.

"Where do you suppose they were after going?" Bekner said.

"We're in a party town on a Saturday night," Whizzfiddle grumbled, motioning to the window. "Where do you think they're going?"

"I don't see Gungren as one who would frequent taverns," Zel said.

"Street magic," Whizzfiddle replied.

He wanted to be out there with them, but he was too busy doing this damned awful thing called "work." The thought made him shiver.

"Should we go after them?" Orophin asked.

Whizzfiddle shook his head.

"They'll just find some other way out."

## AN UNEXPECTED VISITOR

reneth had his feet on the ottoman as he leaned back into his leather chair. He swirled the juice in his glass, taking the occasional taste in celebration of his position on the council.

Saturday evenings were reserved for relaxation. It was a time to reflect on the week's events and see how things progressed on his plans. Rimpertuz was scheduled away as usual, likely spending a less-than-quiet evening with Muppy and her friends.

*Friends*, Treneth thought and scoffed. *Who needs friends when you have power?*

He set the glass on the side table and folded his hands in his lap. It was the first time in years that he had gone more than a few hours without wearing his leather gloves.

He looked at his fingernails and grunted. They were long. They had to be in order to stuff enough... essence... to give him full power when needed.

A knock came at the door.

Treneth stood up and straightened his clothing.

He opened the door and then looked down.

"Councilman Ibork?"

"We need to talk."

## WE HAVE A WINNER!

*G*ungren had followed Winchester and Yultza through various alleys until they finally slipped into one of the taverns that they called a "night club." He had no interest in that. It was all the lights and shops that had him mesmerized.

"Step on up, my boy!"

He looked up at a human who was standing by an odd machine. It had a silver base that was connected to a mini tower with what appeared to be a bell on top. Next to it was a hammer.

Gungren looked from side to side and then finally pointed at himself.

"Yes, you." The man waved him over. "You look like a strong lad, but I'm not sure if you're strong enough. Do you think you're strong enough?"

"What for?"

"Why, to knock the ball up to the bell, my boy."

Gungren rubbed his chin, trying to mimic what he'd seen Whizzfiddle do when he was thinking about something. The distance from the ball to the bell was probably about twenty feet. The ball would be weighted, no doubt, but he wasn't worried about that. While he no longer possessed the full strength he'd had as a giant, he was still ten times stronger than the demographic for this game.

"Okay."

"Two silvers, son," the man said, putting out his hand.

"You pay me two silvers to hit the bell?"

"No. You pay *me* two silvers so you can *try* to hit the bell."

"Why'd I do that?"

The man stepped down from his podium and knelt beside Gungren.

"See that sign, my boy?" He pointed up to a large green board. "If you hit the bell, you can choose whatever you want from that list."

"Magic set," Gungren said softly, his eyes widening.

"What is it you would want?"

"Magic—"

"Magic set it is, then," the man said and sprang back to his podium. "Ladies and gentlemen," he yelled out, "and everything in between, step right up and see if our little man here can hit the bell! He's putting three silver—"

"Two!" Gungren said.

"Ah, yes, two silver on his chances. If he wins, the lad gets a magic set."

People gathered around and started to cheer for Gungren. He liked the attention. Giants were notorious for being solo creatures, but the attention made him feel important.

He picked up the hammer and looked the contraption up and down. About a quarter of the way up was a little silver lever that he didn't recall seeing the first time he'd looked. It sat above a painting of a red rose.

"How many chance I get?" Gungren said. "I not think I try too hard on first chance. I just try for that flower first time."

The man beamed at the crowd.

"Our contestant wants to take a practice swing," he jeered.

The crowd laughed.

"Do you all think he can at least hit the flower?"

The crowd grew even larger.

"They believe in you, my lad!"

The man reached under the podium and Gungren surveyed the unit again to find the metal piece had moved back out of sight.

"Okay," the man said. "You may try for that flower now. It should be a pretty simple hit for a powerful lad such as yourself."

The crowd began chanting the word "flow-er" over and over.

Gungren swung the hammer over his shoulder and let it set for a second. He made sure there were no additional levers the rest of the way up.

With a quick slam, he crushed the mallet on the platform. The ball flew up so fast that it shattered upon hitting the bell.

There was a moment of silence. Then the crowd roared and pooled around him, slapping him on the back and telling him how impressed they were with his strength.

"You cheated me," the man at the podium yelled over the noise.

"I want magic set now," Gungren replied.

"I do not award prizes to cheaters."

"How do I cheated?"

"You cheated by tricking me into removing...I mean, you knew that..." The man stumbled for the right words. "Well...that is to say...you see...it's...um..."

A rough-looking man walked out of the crowd and approached the podium. Gungren assumed it was a werewolf. He was very hairy, had large teeth, and a partially elongated jaw. Gungren looked up at the moon and saw that it wasn't quite full, which explained why the guy was between full-wolf and non-wolf.

The werewolf flexed a set of enormous muscular arms, cracked his neck a few times, and then looked down at the proprietor.

"Give him the prize," he quite literally growled, "or I'll ring that bell with your head."

A short time later the crowd hoorayed again as Gungren walked away with a brand new magic set.

# TIME TO MOVE

*W*hizzfiddle had spent most of the night on the terrace. He found the night air, rank as it was, kept his mind off Benpo's ale. The next time he was in town he planned to use a much stronger spell of protection before going drinking with Curdles.

The terrace afforded him a 180-degree view of Dakmenhem. Rows of buildings stretched as far as the eye could see in one direction, and boats of all shapes and sizes littered the waters in the other.

It was even more awesome now that the sun glittered off the distant ripples.

If he were forced to leave his life of magic in the Upperworld, Whizzfiddle could see himself spending a few hundred years practicing here.

The thought was rather appealing.

For now, though, there were a few people counting on him. If nothing else, he couldn't let them down. At least not without a fight.

He sighed and pushed his creaking bones off the lounge

chair, refilled his backpack and flask, and headed out into the main room.

Zel, Beckner, and Orophin were eating snacks from a box that sat near the window. Whizzfiddle groaned. That would be another couple of gold. The prices trolls charged for the smallest treats were a crime.

He pushed open Gungren's door after telling the others to gather Winchester and Yultza.

"Make it difficult," he pointed out to Bekner.

Gungren wasn't in his bed, but the contents of his pack were spilled out over it. There was a little box with dice and cards and various booklets, and there was a larger book that brought a sense of nostalgia to the old wizard.

*Blitlaray's Guide to Wizardry.*

The leather cover was slightly torn and the binding was creased. He flipped it open and thumbed through a few pages. There were little marks in the margins. He wondered if they had belonged to Gungren or some previous owner.

A giant that could read was odd enough, Whizzfiddle thought, but one that's a wizard? Nonsensical, he added to himself with a frown.

"Gungren," Whizzfiddle called out, "are you here?"

"I are here," a muffled voice replied from the closet.

Whizzfiddle shook his head.

"I *am* here."

Gungren stepped out of the closet, fastening a belt around his robe. "I can see you am here."

"I can see you *are* here," Whizzfiddle corrected.

"Okay," Gungren said at length. "It good that you can see I are here."

"It's good that you can see I *am* here!"

Gungren squinted. "Maybe you am a great wizard, but you got issues."

"Maybe you *are* a great wizard."

"I are?"

"I *am*!"

"I said that you am," Gungren said, looking confused.

"No, it's..." Whizzfiddle slammed his mouth shut and breathed slowly out of his nose as he tapped his finger on the bedpost.

"Never mind. Are you ready to go?"

"Yep," Gungren said.

The little giant walked over and shoved all his junk into the pack.

"I are ready."

"I *am* ready," Whizzfiddle wailed as he exited the room.

"Obviously you am ready," Gungren yelled back. "Elsewise, why you buggin' me!"

## RIMPERTUZ REPORTS

*a*s Treneth worked on his morning tea and toast, he thought over Ibork's request for an alliance.

For the most part, Ibork was a dimwitted fool with a big mouth. But there was something to having a balanced front on the council. Zotrinder would never cross Muppy, and the Croomplatt twins represented their town specifically. They had no designs on power-plays.

A shadow filled the doorway.

"Good morning, Rimpertuz."

"Good day, sir."

"I trust your evening was pleasant?"

"The shipment to Kek has arrived, sir."

Treneth found Rimpertuz's lack of response amusing.

"Excellent," he said after a moment.

It didn't ensure success, but it would delay Whizzfiddle even further. If nothing else, Treneth would make life hard on his former master. Now that Treneth sat on the council he would eventually work the old wizard out of his status. For now the more difficulty Whizzfiddle faced, the happier Treneth would feel.

"I'm sure Farmer Idoon will be much pleased with your gesture of friendship."

Rimpertuz nodded, not smiling.

"You seem distant, Rimpertuz. I trust you are well?"

"Is there anything else I can do for you today, sir?"

Treneth sipped at his tea.

"There is," he said. "It says in today's paper that there is a livestock auction happening at Dappenhibby's Farm. I would like you to see if there are any solid-looking ostriches there for purchase."

"Mr. Dappenhibby doesn't usually raise ostriches, sir."

"Yes, I know," Treneth said, "but I have requested he do so for the last few years, so having a presence there may assist him in future decisions."

"It's a half-day's travel, sir."

"Mmm-hmmm," Treneth agreed, sipping more tea. "I would begin my trip soon then, if I were you."

## THE SHIPMENT ARRIVES

*P*eapod Pecklesworthy awoke to a nice beam of sunshine that peeked through his bedroom curtains.

He loved Sunday mornings.

The townspeople in Kek made it a general rule to celebrate the week's end so heavily on Saturday night that they had a viable excuse to miss Sunday morning services. One would imagine this would have been highly offensive to the local clergyman, but he had often purchased the first round.

Pecklesworthy rarely partook in the festivities as he preferred to keep a clear head and awake early since it was the only time of the week that he could walk the streets in peace. For some reason, the people of Kek saw a wizard as a doctor, lawyer, and any number of things that they found themselves incapable of comprehending. This gave him only Sunday mornings to move about freely. Those few who would be milling about on Sundays were typically of right-enough mind to leave him alone anyway.

He swung his feet off the bed and went about his morning ritual.

He stretched from side to side, did a few deep-knee bends, touched his toes, and worked in a couple of upper-torso twists. He swiveled his head all about to extend his neck for mobility. The wizard had learned a number of exercises when he was an apprentice. He found it cleared his mind and prepared his body for the day.

If there was one thing Pecklesworthy prided himself on, it was discipline and mental fortitude.

He despised work as much as the next wizard, to be sure, but his leisure practices were not of the lazy sort. He would read various philosophies and engage in heated debates on most any topic. Games of wit and cunning were at the top of his list of loves.

Pecklesworthy walked to the window to finalize his morning practice. Taking a deep, cleansing breath, he closed his eyes and flung open the curtains to let the sunlight bathe his face.

The warmth flowed in as he slowly exhaled with an "oooh" sound.

His mind sharpened and he visualized the light immersing his body in its golden potency, filling him from his feet to the top of his head.

The sensation connected him to the world.

It grounded him.

At the end of his morning routine, there was little that could break through Peapod Pecklesworthy's mental fortress.

He opened his eyes and looked out along his property.

There, strewn across his front yard, sat bushel upon bushel of un-shucked pea pods.

"Oh dear."

# THE WAY OF THE SALESPERSON

*C*iven Station was unlike the other stations.

The ceilings were about thirty feet high and the layout was square. It had no shops or restaurants, though there was a pretzel vendor on the east side and a hot dog vendor on the west side. To the south stood the maintenance bays and a plethora of boxes. The north housed a large security base that served as the nexus for all the portals. With all the guards milling about, there was never a fear of being mugged in Civen Station.

"Let's move," the wizard said. "We have a tight timetable."

"Remember our first stop, wizard," Winchester said.

Whizzfiddle bridled a bit but grunted an acknowledgment.

He had agreed to a quick detour into Xarpney. It was not something the wizard looked forward to, but a deal was a deal. They still had a few weeks left to complete the quest, so a few hours wasn't awful. Fortunately, he had stopped off at the bank in Dakmenhem after leaving the hotel...just in case.

He'd toyed with the idea of leaving the others in Civen Station. It would be safer, since they could easily get into mischief in Xarpney. But in Xarpney he would be able to keep an eye on them. No, he decided finally. Best not to risk it.

"Gather around," Whizzfiddle said. "Our friend Winchester must make a stop in a town called Xarpney before we can continue our mission."

Orophin shook his head. "Delaying us again, Winchester?"

"Don't look at me like that," Winchester responded, crossing his arms.

"I want to set clear that Xarpney is an interesting town," Whizzfiddle continued. "It is a town full of people who…sell things."

After a few moments of silence, Bekner said, "What things are they after selling?"

"Everything and anything," Whizzfiddle said. "They're extremely good at it. It's all they do."

"A town full of salespeople?"

Whizzfiddle nodded distantly.

"I've been there," Zel said. "I'd rather visit the vampire town than go back."

"I'm for that," Orophin said dreamily.

Whizzfiddle entered in their destination as everyone assembled on the platform. His finger hovered over the green button, but he stopped and turned back to them.

"There are a few rules we have to follow in Xarpney," he said. "The first rule is that we do not make eye contact with anyone. Doing so opens the door to allow them to ask if you if you need anything. Some will ask this anyway. If they do, simply tell them you are just browsing."

"Is there stores there?" Gungren asked.

"Everything in Xarpney is a store," Whizzfiddle answered. "They'll sell you the shoes right off their feet if you make a reasonable enough offer."

He looked about to make sure that sank in.

"The second rule is that you don't wave at anyone. I know this sounds odd. Many will wave at you as if in greeting, but the moment you wave back you have entered a non-verbal agreement telling them that you wish to inquire about purchasing some item. This ropes you in to a demonstration at the very least."

"Can't you just tell them it was a simple hello?" Orophin said.

"In any other land, yes," Whizzfiddle said. "In Xarpney, everything is about sales, and their local laws support it. So, don't wave."

"Is that it?" Bekner asked.

"Not quite," Whizzfiddle answered. "The last one is the most important. Never, never, *never*...under *any* circumstances, smile at anyone."

Blinks all around, except for Winchester, who tapped his foot impatiently.

"If you smile, you have effectively agreed to a full presentation."

The blinking continued.

"That means you will be subjected to sitting in a room with multiple salespeople, all of whom are trying to push any and all products upon you until you break down and buy something...or, worse, everything! A person could easily go broke in a town like Xarpney."

He allowed the point to sink in.

"Any questions?"

There were none.

With a quick nod to The Twelve, Whizzfiddle pressed the portal button and the troop was swallowed up in the transit system. A moment later the world came back into view.

It was quite a sight.

Xarpney was a business district full of tall glass buildings and bustling walkways. Suits and briefcases were the norm, and almost everyone had a TalkyThingy attached at the ear. There were humans, orcs, ogres, etc. Race didn't matter. A salesperson was a salesperson.

Whizzfiddle had never seen a dwarf, giant, or gorgan in Xarpney, but that didn't mean they weren't on the payroll somewhere. Frankly, he didn't rightly care. He just wanted to get this over with.

"Point two-seven on Appendix B should be amended—" one passerby said as he pushed through the crowd.

"If he won't buy at wholesale there's not a lot I can do—" another said.

It was a world of deals and high-paced finance. One had to be very cautious to avoid getting eaten alive.

"Hello there," Winchester said to a lady who had just shut her TalkyThingy down.

"Good day to you," she said. "Nice day for a purchase, wouldn't you say?"

"I would indeed," Winchester replied.

Whizzfiddle moaned and waved at the others to look at their feet.

"Ah, hello there, good man," a gentlemen in a dark brown suit said. "What can I do for you today?"

"Huh?" Whizzfiddle looked at the man and saw him waving. He looked at his own hand. "Oh." He smiled apologetically. "No, I wasn't waving at you, my good man."

The man smiled back.

"Damn," Whizzfiddle said, recognizing that he had broken all three rules within moments of their arrival.

His shoulders slumped.

"Lead on," Whizzfiddle said to the man.

The interior of the building they had entered was as slick as its exterior. Clean lines and starkly contrasted colors set the tone for what was to come. Presentations. It even smelled business-y.

"Listen to me," Whizzfiddle whispered to his party. "Be careful what you buy. They'll take you for everything you've got. You must be on your guard at all times."

"You're the one who looked at them," Orophin said.

"You also waved at them," Zel pointed out.

"Aye, and then smiled."

"That was a misunderstanding," Whizzfiddle said. "I was trying to stop you lot from...well...this."

"Good work," Gungren said.

Zel seemed like he was about to say something more, but Whizzfiddle gave him a stern enough glance that the former knight was compelled to move to the other side of Bekner.

Winchester and Yultza were on their own. Whizzfiddle wasn't worried about the former dragon. The salespeople would have to watch their backs around him.

But the rest had him concerned. Zel would break within minutes, if not sooner. Gungren was probably already planning his next purchase—something related to magic, no doubt. Bekner and Orophin were the only two who had a chance of pushing through this without too much of a fuss.

"Now then," the man whomWhizzfiddle had smiled at said, "if you'll each move into one of these rooms—"

"We'd like to stay together," the elderly wizard stated.

"Ah, so you're looking to broker a deal for a business, then?"

"Well, no."

"Are you incorporated in some way? Maybe investors?"

"Not exactly."

The man tapped his foot and checked his watch.

"We're on a quest, you see."

"Unfortunately," the businessman said, "we have no set process for managing questing parties. So if you'll each choose a room, someone will be along shortly to provide you a presentation, build a deal, and then get you on your way. Remember, a good deal is only good when everyone is happy with the outcome!"

Whizzfiddle grunted. More like when you walk out broke and they walk out with a commission high enough to pay for a year's rent.

"You have to buy something," he whispered as they parted. "Just be wary."

His blood pressure began to rise. There was nothing worse than suffering through a sales presentation, except, possibly, working.

Whizzfiddle was doing both.

## TRENETH CONCERNED

reneth had only once before visited Madam Slaygun. She was a seer, a practice he found akin to cheating. At first he had lobbied for her type to be classified as non-magical workers so they wouldn't be allowed guild access. His proposition was unanimously refused, though he was promised they would not be allowed to look into the future. Nor could they "spy" on anyone unless paid to do so. And, finally, they would not be granted the status of wizard.

From that point on, Treneth had endeavored to keep his life cloaked, which explained why he had visited her the first time. He needed to find out how well his protection spells held up against someone viewing him.

When Treneth had first met her, he had assumed she had been alive since the dawn of time. The gray streaks in her ratty nest of hair alone made her look ancient, but it was her missing teeth, and lack of dentures, that really gave her that "old hag" look.

The fact was, though, that Treneth was twice her age.

Regardless of her lacking visual appeal, Teggins was out

215

of the picture, so Treneth had to choose between being blind about Whizzfiddle's progress or to cheat a little. He finally came to the conclusion that he would not sleep well without some ongoing status.

"Xarpney?" Treneth said.

"That's what I am reading, yes."

"Why would they go there? Why would *anyone* go there?"

"Best deals," Madam Slaygun said. "Brutal place, yes, but they have everything. What they don't have, they can get."

Treneth thought about that for a moment. It was true. Whatever you needed, someone in Xarpney could hook it up. Or could they?

Wizard spells were tricky things, Treneth mused. They were tied directly to the caster, except in certain circumstances where a third-party has requested that they be the owner of the spell, which is a rare instance and usually involves a cheating spouse and some sort of chastity device. Spells the magnitude of transfiguration could not be placed onto another, unless the other was also a wizard of similar aptitude. Further, this type of spell was permanent if not undone in time. The lifeline of the casting wizard became moot because those suffering the morphism learn to accept the new identity. That accession acts as a binding agent.

Still...

"You don't know of any wizards down there powerful enough to counter transfiguration, do you?"

"To take on someone else's undoing spell?" she replied. "I think I would have caught a rumor or two over someone like that."

"My feeling too," Treneth said. "Can you see what's going to happen next?"

"You of all people should know that's not allowed, per the rules of the guild."

He nodded.

"I lost the connection," Madam Slaygun said. "Xarpney is a hassle because of the constant stream of TalkyThingy signals flowing this way and that."

Treneth leaned back.

"No matter," he said. "I at least know where he is for now. I shall come back in a few days to check on him again. If you can keep tabs on him, I will make sure you are well paid."

"No, I don't think I can do that."

"I assure you I can afford—"

"It's not about the money, Treneth," Madam Slaygun said. "It's about what you're doing with Master Whizzfiddle. He's a friend of mine and I know what you're up to. Everyone knows what you're up to."

Treneth stood up and tightened his gloves. He walked to the door and stopped.

"According to the guild rules, a wizard must endeavor to serve those in need, Madam Slaygun."

"According to the very same guild rules, a seer is not afforded the classification of wizard. If I'm not mistaken, that was entered into the books on account of one Treneth of Dahl."

"You must still follow the rules of the guild!"

"Only those rules specifically denoted for seers," Madam Slaygun replied with a smile. "Do note I am well versed in what can and cannot be condemning to my position. For example, I *am* allowed to have relations with an apprentice in the guild, so you may by all means have young Rimpertuz pay me a visit any evening that you wish. It is one hundred percent allowed, according to guild rules, and it's one hundred percent desired, according to me."

Treneth was in complete shock. He could not contain the look on his face. Had she somehow broken through his shields? He had spent weeks toiling through books, concoctions, and incantations to protect himself.

"So it's true that you set Muppy up," she said, giggling. "I'd heard the rumor, but I wasn't sure." She stopped. "Ah, you probably thought I was spying on you, knowing your paranoid little mind. But, my dear, *that* would be illegal unless I had been paid to do so, and I assure you that I was not."

His mouth was still hanging open as he closed the door.

# WHAT DID YOU GET?

*W*hizzfiddle left the presentation feeling numb. He almost found himself missing the guild meetings in comparison. Even one of Zotrinder's speeches could have soothed his aching ears at the moment.

Everyone else was in the waiting room, which meant he'd held out the longest. It was obvious the moment he saw them that they had all succumbed in one way or another to the pressure.

Even Yultza looked a fair bit different. Not that she was his problem. Still, whatever it was that was different, it was good.

"Nice walking staff," Whizzfiddle said to Gungren. "I'm surprised they had one in your size. Too bad it will be naught more than a throwing stick when you've returned to your normal stature."

Gungren seemed oblivious to the remark.

"I got a new book too," he said, pointing to a fresh copy of *Master Carbigue's Transfiguration Nation*.

Orophin was no longer in his elven clothes. He now

sported a dark suit with a silk fluffy shirt. Whizzfiddle shook his head.

"You should know better," he said and then turned to Bekner. "What happened to you?"

"I tried getting around them," Bekner said, "but they're a crafty bunch."

"Are you wearing a sports jersey?"

"Aye," Bekner said, snapping his fingers and pointing at Zel. "That's what they were after calling this thing. I couldn't remember the name for the life of me." He turned his back a bit. "Has me name on it and everything."

"I see that, yes," Whizzfiddle said. "The question is, why?"

"As to that, it seems that I'm after being one of the taller people they've seen. The man says he wants to be my agent or something of the sort. I don't know what an agent is, but he said there'd be money. Gold too," Bekner added with a smile. "Lots of gold."

Whizzfiddle peered closer, leaning forward and examining Bekner's teeth.

"Is that a gold tooth?"

Bekner slammed his mouth shut. "Um," he said, shifting a bit, "aye."

"This wouldn't have anything to do with a game where you put a ball through the air and into a hoop, would it?"

"Aye," Bekner said, eyes widening. "You know about it?"

"You do realize that when you're back here,"—Whizzfiddle put his hand at about waist height—"you'll be more useful as the ball, right?"

Bekner's face contorted for a moment and then went back to thoughtful. Without a word, he pulled the jersey off and shoved it into one of his pockets.

Whizzfiddle turned his attention to Zel. He studied him for a few moments but couldn't spot any changes. If anyone was to fall to the pressure, it would be the former knight. Then he saw it. A look of discomfort. A bit of angst.

"Tight-cut underwear?" Whizzfiddle said.

"Damn no," Zel blurted with what only could be described as an angry look.

The wizard blinked in surprise.

"What did they do to you?"

"Hell damn, old man," Zel said. "I don't have to answer that."

"'Hell damn?'" Whizzfiddle looked over at Orophin. "What is going on here?"

"They gave him tough-guy pills," the elf said.

"I don't need you sharing my business, damned elf."

"Watch it," Orophin said, glaring.

Zel snuck behind Bekner but held up the same finger that often got Whizzfiddle in trouble.

Whizzfiddle rolled his eyes.

"So he talks tough, but he's still afraid of everything?"

"I'm not afraid of a damn thing, old man," Zel said, peeping around Bekner.

Bekner reached back and pulled the knight forward as easily as a giant could lift a pebble. He brought Zel up to face height.

"Drop the pills," Bekner growled.

"Hell damn," Zel croaked as the bottle struck the floor, followed by the piddle of his bladder's contents.

Whizzfiddle marched the container over to the sales desk and threw them in the trash, muttering how the Xarpniens should be ashamed of themselves. He nearly requested an audience with a supervisor, but he didn't want to chance another round of presentations. The pills would wear off eventually. Until then, it was time to go.

"Don't you want to know what I did?" Winchester asked.

"Not really," Whizzfiddle said as he directed everyone to

put on their "I've been sold!" stickers. "It's because of you that we now have a snazzily dressed elf, a dwarf who expects to be a famous basketball player, a giant who has furthered his desire to be a wizard, and a...knight...who uses foul language."

"What about the great wizard, then?" Winchester asked. "Was he able to refrain in stoic manner?"

Whizzfiddle huffed and pushed out the door.

He made a direct line for the nearest portal complex as the disappointed faces of salespeople caught their "I've been sold!" badges. It was difficult to get through the crowd of vultures until Bekner took the lead. Something about a seven-foot, thick-as-a-rock, beardless cave-dweller with a purposeful stride told even the most tenacious Xarpnien that another group of potentials would be along soon.

"What did them get?" Gungren said to Winchester.

"*I* didn't get anything," the lizard replied from atop Yultza's shoulder. He pointed at Yultza's breasts and said, "Magic."

"She got magic thingums?"

Winchester laughed.

Whizzfiddle did not. It didn't matter to him what Yultza did. She wasn't part of the undoing group. Still, he sneaked a peek as Yultza cupped them and said "bigger." Sure enough, magic boobs. The elderly wizard wasn't as driven by such things at his age, but he could still appreciate the dynamic and made a mental note to pick up a copy of *PlayDragon* upon its release.

"Nice, aren't they?" Winchester said to the wizard.

Whizzfiddle averted his attention and slammed directly into Bekner's back. Winchester and Yultza laughed.

"See?" Winchester said as Whizzfiddle rubbed his nose. "I told you those things held power."

Whizzfiddle moved past Bekner and worked over the

console. He set the destination for Kek and verified everyone was on the platform. Soon this adventure would be over and he could go back to his daily routine. One more day, he thought. Two at most.

"What the damn hell did you buy anyway?" Zel asked with his hand firmly in the air.

Whizzfiddle's finger hovered over the green button.

"Timeshare."

KEK IN FLAMES

*I*t was late afternoon when they arrived in Kek.

Something was odd about the city. It did not look as Whizzfiddle remembered it.

The last time he had visited was almost a hundred years prior, but back then it was a quaint little town that sat nestled in the hills. His memory pulled forth the picturesque vision that now blanketed the covers of many greeting cards. It had been such a breathtaking view that Whizzfiddle had commissioned a painting be made of it. The resultant portrait was now framed and hanging in his den.

"I don't recall the town billowing smoke," Whizzfiddle said.

"The hell damn fires are also out of place," Zel responded.

"Is there a war going on in the north that we were unaware of?"

"No, Orophin," Whizzfiddle said. "This is not caused by a war. This is magic."

"How you tell that?" Gungren said.

"I have my ways."

"Aye," Bekner said, pointing in the direction that

Whizzfiddle was looking. "He sees the guards over there carrying out a wizard, he does."

They ran down to the guards and Whizzfiddle made out Pecklesworthy's dangling form as he was aloft on the shoulders of angry-looking sentinels. The wizard's arms were flopping this way and that and he was blathering something about the habitual patterns of rosebushes during the doomcupper mating season. Whizzfiddle had no idea what a doomcupper was, but it was clearly of some import to the bedazzled Pecklesworthy.

"Pardon me," Whizzfiddle said. Everyone eyed him suspiciously. "Is he well?"

"You ever heard of a doomcupper?" one of the men asked.

"No," Whizzfiddle replied. "Actually, I was just wondering what it was. I assumed it to be something indigenous to Kek."

"It's not," another man chimed in as they kept walking away. "Rosebushes ain't got no habits that I know about."

Another soldier moved toward Whizzfiddle, looked over everyone, stopping on Zel for a moment, and then sat on a log and broke out a cigar.

"You Whizzfiddle?" the soldier said.

"I am. And you are?"

"Sergeant Ward," he answered. "We heard you'd be on your way."

"Is that so?"

The sergeant took a drag from the cigar and nodded.

"May I ask by whom?"

"You may."

"Okay then, by—"

"Let's just say that we try to keep tabs on portal usage in our area," Ward interjected. He squinted and pointed at Zel. "Your man there knows what I'm talking about."

The knight mumbled something about how hell should

be damned. Soldiers kept tabs on the portals. Whizzfiddle had this memory filed away under "who cares?"

"So what happened here?"

"Pea pod shipment came in yesterday," Ward said, flicking an ash. "We figured it was just the town wizard setting up for the cold season. Didn't know he had some type of problem."

All wizards knew that Pecklesworthy was an obsessive-compulsive. If he saw an un-shucked pea pod, he had to shuck it. He couldn't resist. But Pecklesworthy knew well his own addictive nature and there was no way he would have ordered a large shipment of pea pods unless he was ready to end it all.

This smelled like the work of Treneth.

"How much came in?" Whizzfiddle asked.

"A few carriages full, I'd say."

Whizzfiddle groaned and plunked down on the log. Ward offered him a cigar, but he refused and instead grabbed his flask.

Kek's partial demise made sense now. Unable to contain himself, Pecklesworthy would have shucked like mad and his power would have overflowed until he lost his mind. Without anyone of equal strength to contain him, the poor man would begin to launch spells uncontrollably until he either combusted or went into the mental equivalent of la-la land.

Pecklesworthy shucking a few carriages full of pea pods would be like Whizzfiddle drinking ten kegs of Gilly's ale. It would be amazing if Pecklesworthy ever gained his sanity back.

"How many people died?"

"Nobody, that we're aware of," Ward said and then stood up and brushed off his pants. "Everyone was sleeping in on account of it being Sunday and the only thing that Pecklesworthy really hit was some trees, an empty warehouse, and the church. Nobody goes to the church on a Sunday."

"Not even the preacher?"

"Especially not the preacher."

"Oh."

Whizzfiddle looked over the city and clicked his teeth.

"You're welcome to stay, of course. But I sense what you've come for has completely lost his mind."

"Is he going to prison?" Whizzfiddle asked.

"After blowing up the church he'll probably be elected mayor, but that won't happen until he regains his mind. The man is completely batty right now."

"Where then?"

"There is a witch outside of town—"

"Glinayeth Noosebaum," Whizzfiddle interjected, remembering the lady well. She was one of the best healers in all of the Upperworld. But even she wouldn't be able to bring poor Pecklesworthy back from such a state for many years, and that meant that this little quest was in dire jeopardy.

"Gentlemen," Ward said with a nod before he began walking back down the path to the city.

The canopy of smoke and the blathering Pecklesworthy foretold Whizzfiddle's next thousand years.

There was no way to get these lads back to their old selves with Pecklesworthy out of commission. Treneth had succeeded. In order to do it, his former apprentice had had to resort to destroying a fellow wizard's capacity to contain his own drool, but Treneth had won this round.

"What will we do now?" Orophin said.

"I'm sorry, lads," Whizzfiddle replied, wanting to pull out a full keg and drink enough to join Pecklesworthy.

"Sorry?" Zel said, stepping forward. "Damn hell, old man. I can't live throughout my days like this!"

*Zel's not even shaking*, Whizzfiddle thought. Interesting. Maybe he shouldn't have thrown out the pills after all.

"Since that done," Gungren said, joining Whizzfiddle on the log, "you teach me wizard stuff?"

Whizzfiddle exhaled and shrugged. Only card-carrying guild members were allowed to master an apprentice. That, at least, was one plus of losing his status.

"We're after having a contract," Bekner said. "You can't back out now."

Winchester scuttled into the mix and shushed everyone.

"It's not that easy, you big oaf," he said, "and he can't be your master if he's not in the guild, Gungren."

He paced back and forth, making little footprints in the dirt.

"I have an idea," Winchester said. "It will be unpopular, but it'll be better than continuing your lives as you are." He gazed at Whizzfiddle. "You're the only one who can call on them at this point, wizard. I fell out of favor when I usurped my father's den."

Whizzfiddle stopped mid-drink and slowly lowered the bottle. It *was* an option, but not one to take lightly. Of course he was just about to drink himself into that domain anyway.

"I'll have to pull in favors," he said.

"Probably a good many," Winchester agreed.

"Why are you really doing this?" Whizzfiddle said.

Winchester shrugged. "Right thing to do."

"Doubtful," Whizzfiddle scoffed. "It's a valid idea, nonetheless."

"Excuse me," Orophin spoke up. "I don't want to interfere in this delectable conversation, but how about letting us in on the secret?"

"Afterlife," Whizzfiddle answered and then took another swig.

"Hell damn."

"As in where people go when they die?"

"No, as in where people go when they ascend," Winchester said. "People who die go somewhere else," he added vaguely.

"Where?" Gungren asked.

"Depends on which of the damn Twelve you follow," Zel answered and then he snatched Whizzfiddle's flask and took a gulp.

"I are not following any."

"Then ye'll not be after going anywhere," Bekner said.

"Oh."

Whizzfiddle took his flask back and pointed at Zel sternly. The pills didn't really cure the knight's issues, they just made him a jerk.

"Can we skip the religious discussion for a minute?" Winchester said. "Whizzfiddle, you can get us there."

"You need something, Winchester," Whizzfiddle accused.

"So do you."

"True," Whizzfiddle agreed. "Okay," he said as he pulled himself up, staggering a bit. The booze was infiltrating nicely. "This is only going to work if we all agree."

"To die?"

"Yes, Orophin."

"Not me," Gungren said. "I want be a wizard."

"Not going to happen without a master," Winchester said. "The guild won't accept you."

"I go if Whizzfiddle agree."

"No," Whizzfiddle said immediately. "I will not take on a new apprentice."

"Then I not go."

They were in a stalemate, listening to the rustling of leaves and the distant shouts of the townsfolk. The juxtaposition of nature and man's destruction was humbling.

Whizzfiddle saw a walking path and headed toward it, putting his hand out to stop the others from following.

"Stay put," he commanded them. "I need to think."

He could force the little giant, with a little help anyway, but his ethic forbade such an action. He could accept Gungren as an apprentice, with a lot of booze, but his lack of work-ethic jolted at the concept.

He stopped walking and leaned heavily on the staff. Maybe it was time to retire. His bones had been creaking for two-thirds of his life. They weren't any worse now than six hundred years ago, but they weren't exactly great then. He'd seen it all in the magic world, too. No, he'd not run *every* type of quest, but it was simple enough to get the gist of any type of magic. The name "Whizzfiddle" didn't appear all that often in wizarding circles anymore either, except as an example of what not to do on certain occasion. There was no fire for the profession, only fear of losing it.

"Yes," he said aloud. "Maybe."

He had more than enough money. Enough to last him hundreds of years anyway. That would give him time to find a new profession or to invest in such a way to extend that money even further.

The troop was arguing in the distance. Try as he might, he couldn't shut them out.

Maybe the giant would make a good apprentice. It was possible. Gungren could be the first giant to ever become a wizard. That was something to hang your hat on, assuming you didn't have a head of mood hair. "You're the Master Wizard who trained the giant?" people would say. Then they'd probably kick his rear end and ask what he had been thinking.

"Nice chap," Whizzfiddle mused to the tree he was admiring. "Brighter than any giant I've ever seen."

On the face of it that wasn't saying much.

Then he added, "Brighter than most humans too."

"Someone is smart," the tree said.

"Yes," Whizzfiddle agreed. "Likable too, though he's a bit annoying."

"Everyone is."

"Likable?"

"No, annoying."

Whizzfiddle nodded and pinched the bridge of his nose to stave off a sneeze. He failed.

"The Twelve has your back," the tree said in normal sneeze-response etiquette.

"Thank you, and don't think I haven't noticed that you are a talking tree."

"Many people just assume they've gone off the deep end," the tree said.

"I'm sure it's the booze," Whizzfiddle argued. "In my years, I've talked with rocks, trees, water, and even my toenail, though he hasn't spoken to me since I told him he looked to have a fungus problem."

He tipped back the alembic and drained the final drops.

"Sad, really. We used to have the best debates."

"Toes can be formidable," the tree said. "Or, uh, so I've heard. Hard to say, you know, not having toes and all."

Whizzfiddle sat down and leaned up against the trunk.

"Mind?"

"No," the tree said. "I have little other purpose than standing here all the time. Thank you for not watering me, though."

Whizzfiddle chuckled and closed his eyes.

He missed the days of going on a bender to gain enough power to make inanimate objects start up conversations with him. It was scary at first. So much so that he'd considered giving up drinking entirely. But the conversations were good and enlightening, and the debates, though heated, unfolded interesting tapestries of thought that he was shocked to learn he'd possessed.

"So what will you do?"

"Hmmm? Oh, I don't know," Whizzfiddle said. "I suppose I'll have to take that little pain-in-the-rump on as my pupil. Hate the thought, but I can't let the others down like that."

"Good," the tree said. "I...they will be happy with that."

"I don't know about that. Dying isn't very fun."

"Done it?"

"Well, no," Whizzfiddle said. "Kind of made a career out of avoiding it, but I've seen people who have gone through the process and it didn't look like they would put it on their most-recommended list. You?"

"No," the tree replied, "but I don't fear it. Neither will the others, except maybe Zel."

"Yes...um…" Whizzfiddle got to his feet and looked at the tree. "How do you know about Zel? I didn't mention that name."

"I'm, uh, *you*, remember?"

The voice was familiar. Very familiar.

"Yes," he said and then cantered about in the small clearing. "It's that damn lizard that I worry about. He's a slippery one. Not much brains in there."

"I beg your...I mean, why do you say that?"

Whizzfiddle grinned, facing away from the tree. "Can just tell about some people, you know? Tiny little brains. Cunning, sure, but smart? No."

"Maybe it's just that his aptitude is such that you can't comprehend him."

Whizzfiddle snickered. "I doubt that, tree. He couldn't find his tail with both hands."

"Jealous of him, are you?"

"Yes," Whizzfiddle said formally. "That's probably it. I'm

jealous of him. Especially that obnoxious odor that permeates the air when he is around."

"You're saying that I...erm...that he stinks?"

"I could smell him from a mile away," Whizzfiddle affirmed.

Silence.

"Well," Whizzfiddle said after a few moments. "I guess I have work to do. Thank you for the discussion...tree."

About thirty feet ahead, Whizzfiddle saw Winchester scampering up the path, skirting the edge. No doubt the stench remark would weigh on the lizard's mind for a bit.

The tree did not say its goodbyes.

## NEWS, MUGGINGS, AND MEETINGS

*H*e blew up the whole town?"

It was only logical that Pecklesworthy would overdo it, but Treneth didn't think it would be this bad.

"That's what I heard, sir," Rimpertuz said, pacing back and forth. "Well, mostly the church, but there was a warehouse and some trees too."

Treneth hadn't planned on that. He figured Pecklesworthy might just disappear for a few days and leave Whizzfiddle with even less time to complete his quest. When they were younger, Treneth would see Pecklesworthy streak off into the woods after a pea pod shucking fest. Eventually the wizard would return, looking a bit disheveled and curious about what had happened.

"They said that Master Pecklesworthy was really messed up," Rimpertuz added.

"How did you learn of this?"

"Farmer Idoon said that a pigeon arrived from Kek. The note on its leg explained what had happened."

"I see," Treneth said, thinking that maybe having

TalkyThingy technology in the Upperworld wouldn't be such a bad thing.

"Should we tell the rest of the council, sir?"

"No!" Treneth snapped. "I mean, no. No, we should not. I would not want you to get in trouble, Rimpertuz."

"I don't know what to do, sir."

"It's a horrible affair, to be true. If the council finds out, I would imagine there is a strong chance that you'd spend a great deal of time in prison."

By this time Rimpertuz was nearly hyperventilating. The floorboard was creaking every few moments as the man continued his pacing. Treneth winced with each step but kept himself composed.

"You know," Treneth said thoughtfully, "it's possible that this could be seen as merely an unfortunate happenstance."

"It could?"

"You could say that you were simply sending a thoughtful gift to one of my old acquaintances. That *was* your intent, yes?"

"Yes," Rimpertuz said, brightening. "That's exactly what happened. It was just a present! How was I to know it would cause this problem?"

Treneth smiled. It sealed the deal that Rimpertuz identified the shipment as truly coming from his own hand. Ah, the mind of a wizard.

"Best to keep this from your new acquaintance. We wouldn't want your dear Muppy thinking any less of you, now would we?"

"No, sir!"

He checked his calendar and then his watch. It was almost time to meet up with Ibork.

"I have to run to town, Rimpertuz. Remember to keep this little incident between just the two of us, yes?"

"Absolutely, sir."

Treneth marched off toward Gilly's. The thought of visiting such an establishment twisted his innards, but it was the one place that the other wizards seemed to avoid, apart from Whizzfiddle, and he was nowhere near Rangmoon at the moment.

It would do to take his mind off what he had done to Pecklesworthy, though. Treneth had never even considered that the fool of a wizard would take the shucking this far. Maybe it was for the best, though. If the man couldn't contain himself, he wasn't fit to serve the profession of wizard. Then he remembered that none of the wizards were all that capable in the self-containment department.

He turned his mind back to the task at hand: meeting with Ibork.

The halfling's request of a combined front had made more and more sense as Treneth had mulled it over. Nobody liked Ibork, including Treneth. The fat little man was abhorrent, argumentative, boisterous, and self-involved. He was also somewhat gullible, and that meant Treneth could manipulate the halfling without much effort.

"Excuse me, sir," a rather large man said as Treneth entered one of the alleyways adjacent to the town square.

Treneth studied the man for a moment, noting his rather large size and perfect hair. His choice of clothing labeled him as well-to-do, but Treneth pulled on the cuffs of his gloves to tighten them, just in case.

"Yes?"

"I would like to alleviate that weight from your hip."

Treneth looked at his hip.

"No, the other one."

His change purse hung neatly below the edge of his vest. "Ah, this is a mugging, then?"

"That completely depends on your willingness to

participate. If I have to resort to violence, *then* it would be a mugging."

"I find it odd that someone with your obvious command of civilized language and attendant garb would resort to such thievery."

The man bowed slightly. "I thank you for noticing my eloquence, and I would say that you're quite a fetching fellow yourself. Yes, rather cute indeed."

"Huh?"

"But," the man continued, "it would be better for you to not judge *this* book by its cover. I have little in the way of conscience when it comes to, as you put it, thievery."

"Well, I would not wish to test that assertion," Treneth said as he began to unravel the strap.

He murmured a brief incantation and then handed over the satchel. Immediately the man sank to his knees with a groan.

"It seems," the man said through gritted teeth, "that Teggins left a bit of information out when giving me this mission."

"What was that?"

"I am clearly tangling with a wizard, of sorts."

"Clearly," Treneth replied. "What did you say about Teggins?"

"Teggins?" The man grunted. "Did I say Teggins?"

"I believe you did."

"This is rather painful, you know."

"I do so apologize."

"Can't be helped. One of the dangers of my profession. If you would be ever so kind as to release this pouch from my fingers, I would be most appreciative."

"I think you've already gathered that I'm not that stupid."

"You've my word as a gentleman that I'll neither attack nor scamper off."

"I've never known common criminality was a gentlemanly profession."

"You wound me, sir."

Treneth walked beyond the edge of the alley and whistled out to one of the town guards. The guard looked but didn't move from his post. Sighing, Treneth spoke out another spell and the guard came running.

"Someone will be here to collect you in a moment. Then I'll remove the purse from your hands."

"I would ask that you just release me now. This way I will not hold a grudge against you. I do so have a tendency of doing that, I'll admit."

"I am touched by your concern," Treneth said, "but I think I will chance it. Unless, of course, you would like to elaborate on what you were saying about Teggins."

"Sorry, I haven't the faintest idea what you're talking about," the would-be thief said with a grunt.

"Did Teggins send you up here?" No response. "Your lack of response is indicative that he was involved."

"I've already explained that I know of no Teggins."

"Yet you said his name very clearly just moments ago."

"I believe you may be hearing things, good sir."

"No matter," Treneth said as he heard footsteps approaching. "His message was received. There will be a time when Teggins will have need of something from me. Then our score will be evened."

The guard rounded the corner and took to putting his sword at the ruffian's throat. Treneth took back his satchel and the man stood up, rubbing his hand. At his full height, the thief was easily a head taller than the guard.

"What is your name?" the criminal said.

Treneth did not answer.

"This is Master Wizard Treneth of Dahl," the guard provided.

"He already knows my name, guard," Treneth said. "He got it from Teggins."

"Who's Teggins, sir?" the guard asked.

"Never mind," Treneth answered with a wave of his hand.

"My name is Curlang Jetherby, Treneth of Dahl. Remember it well, wizard, for you'll see me again. Mark my words."

Treneth smiled and said, "I think, to be safe, that you should be relaxed for your trip to your cell. We wouldn't want you overpowering our fine guard here, now would we?"

He flicked his wrist and Curlang staggered a bit.

"Take him away, guard. He shouldn't cause you any trouble for the better part of an hour. I wouldn't dawdle, though, just in case."

The guard walked Curlang toward the city prison as Treneth crossed the town square.

People had a tendency to bow to him whenever he came through. It was one of the many perks of being a wizard. He did rather enjoy it. What he didn't like was entering a tavern, especially not one that looked as shabby as Gilly's.

"Hello, sir," a gap-toothed man said from behind the bar as Treneth walked in.

Treneth sniffed and joined Ibork.

"What'll you gents be having?"

"Ale," Ibork said.

"Do you have any freshly brewed tea?"

"We have ale and stew, sir."

"'No' would be a more succinct response," Treneth pointed out.

"That's right true, sir," the barkeep said, "but when I respond in such a way, people ask what we do have. Two birds, one stone, sir."

Treneth pursed his lips. "Nothing for me, then."

"The stew is good," Ibork said as he patted his sweating forehead with a handkerchief.

"I have decided to accept your proposal, Ibork."

"Excellent, I was thinking that—"

Treneth held up his hand. "There are to be some basic guidelines we will need to follow. There is no point in our butting heads in the future if we can set in motion plans to avoid such unpleasantness, true?"

"Sounds wise," Ibork said, looking as though he had just made his first friend. Ever.

This was going to be too simple, Treneth thought. Ibork was far inferior. Even the dumbest bargainer knows better than to indulge intoxicants until *after* the deal is done.

No matter, all Treneth had to do was set Ibork up so that all the wizards in the land would resent him. It would be easiest with Ibork because he was already disliked. After he was taken care of, Treneth would move on to Zotrinder. One by one, he would discredit them all. That would open the stage for Treneth to take the council chair.

"It seems most prudent to me," Treneth said, "that you should be the council chair."

Ibork almost choked.

"Now, hear me out. Our Muppy is quite capable in some respects, but her recent judgment—or lack thereof—is demonstrative that her first duty is not to the guild. Wouldn't you agree?"

"Entirely."

"I would also go as far as to say that having Zotrinder as her second, should anything happen to her, is a concern that all wizards should share."

"May The Twelve forbid it," Ibork whispered while making a hand gesture that consisted of throwing both hands up, fingers spread, and then dropping the left hand and leaving two fingers up on the right hand.

Treneth leaned forward and looked from left to right. Ibork mirrored the action. It was almost too easy.

"Would it not be better if you were the council chair and Zotrinder was *your* second?"

"It would not, yes."

Treneth squinted. "It wouldn't?"

"Would," Ibork said, patting his forehead again. "I meant that it would be better."

"It will require vigilance, my dear Ibork."

"Oh," Ibork croaked.

# AFTERLIFE SECURITY

$\mathcal{I}$n preparation for sending everyone into the Afterlife, Whizzfiddle had taken enough of his fill of the spirits to knock the wits out of a rhino. He began the incantation a few times. The slurring of words and his inability to focus made the process challenging.

The first attempt resulted in a localized rain shower that soaked them all. The second turned everyone's clothing bright pink. Orophin seemed pleased with this until Whizzfiddle managed to reverse it.

Finally, a light wind started coming in and began swirling around the troop. As it picked up velocity, Whizzfiddle yelled for them to link arms and hold tight. Flashes of light flooded the vortex. Everyone was screaming as they were lifted from the ground. Mostly they were screaming at Zel because his piddle floated in mid-air and hit each of them as they rotated into it. One more flash and a blinding orb appeared in their midst. It grew in heat and intensity until it threatened to rip them to shreds.

Then it suddenly stopped and they fell to the ground.

Whizzfiddle found himself lying on a cold marble floor a

few feet away from a large glass booth. Everything in the room was white and glossy, except for the doors, which were red and dull.

"We're dead?" Zel said.

"Not exactly," Whizzfiddle replied as he got to his feet. His head was clear since most of the booze had been worn off due to the use of its power. "More like in limbo. Our bodies are with us here. If we were dead, we wouldn't all be together."

"Unless we all praised the same god," Winchester added.

The Afterlife was almost identical to real life except that it was always sunny or rainy or snowy or...well, whatever you wanted your personal experience to be. This could present an oddness to newcomers since some people would be wearing heavy coats in what appeared to be the middle of summer, or, conversely, swim trunks in three feet of snow. It was all about perspective.

For Whizzfiddle and his troop, though, they would only experience what actual residences had set as their personal eternities.

"Passports?" an official-looking man in a blue uniform said.

"Ah, yes," Whizzfiddle said, patting his coat pockets before realizing that was pointless since he had no papers with him. "As to that, we're not technically supposed to be here."

"No problem," the man said, gesturing toward a hole in the ground. "If you'll just hop in here we'll get you on your way."

"Sorry," Whizzfiddle said. "We *intend* to be here, but—"

"Everyone *intends* to be here, sir," the man interrupted. "Sadly, only a few actually achieve what they intend. Now, if you would all—"

"Stop," Whizzfiddle commanded, garnering a surprised

look from the guard. "I am Xebdigon Whizzfiddle of the Third Order in the Second Age." He scratched his beard. "Or maybe it's the Second Order in the Third Age. Well, it's definitely some order in some age, that much I well know!"

The man tapped his foot and yawned.

"I have come seeking my former master. It is imperative that I speak with him. This is a matter of grave urgency."

"Considering you're all dead," replied the guard, "I would say the graveness has passed, sir."

Whizzfiddle stumbled at the logic. *True enough*, he thought.

"Yes, well, I need to see Master Blitlaray."

"Ooh," the guard said after a pause. "Seems he's unavailable."

"Master Blitlaray was your master?" Gungren said with a look of sincere admiration.

"Hmmm? Different one."

"Blitlaray is a common name?" Orophin asked.

"Sounds like it's after being unique to my ears."

Whizzfiddle turned on them. "I don't know!" He pushed forward, feeling a bit irritable. "I'm sure there was some novelty to it when I was accepted, but he turned out to be relatively stagnant minded so I made no further fuss. Probably just a cousin or grandson or something." He spun back on the guard. "Try him again."

"Still out," the guard said without a moment's hesitation.

"You're not even trying," Whizzfiddle blurted.

"Aren't you astute? Now, if you would all just hop off this ledge—"

Bekner stepped forward and plucked the man on the back of his head, hard. A resounding snap threw the guard to the ground and he groaned.

Another guard bolted in, looking perplexed. "What's going on here?"

Whizzfiddle moved past Bekner.

"It's all a misunderstanding. This guard was trying to contact Master Blitlaray, and my friend here thought he was pulling a weapon. He's not familiar with your ways, you see."

The guard looked at them dubiously and knelt beside his comrade. He felt the man's neck and then stood back up.

"He's alive," he said and then seemed to think better of it. "I mean, not alive really. You know, I mean he's alive in a manner of speaking."

"Right," Whizzfiddle said. "Good."

"Blitlaray, you said?"

"Indeed, that's correct."

The man consulted a large sheet of names, flipping it over multiple times. "I have a Gesdeegun Blitlaray and a Herbie Blitlaray. I'm assuming you want the former?"

"Herbie, if you would."

"Really?"

"Really."

After a few moments the man turned back and asked for Whizzfiddle's name again. Then he moved off to the main office and got on what appeared to be a TalkyThingy, albeit a more advanced model. There was a lot of nodding and hand gesturing before the man filled out some paperwork and called them over.

"Master Blitlaray...of the Herbie persuasion, will be here shortly to collect all of you."

"Excellent."

"We'll need to get all the paperwork done on you and you'll have to go through the security screening process."

They were led through a set of doors and made to form a line. Everyone had to remove their boots and put all metal items into little plastic containers that they then slid onto a black belt. The items disappeared into some sort of chamber. Then, each in turn walked through a large box with a rotating arm that spun around them, beeped, and opened on the other side.

Gungren had gone first and was now standing beside a man who was looking at a screen that seemed capable of inspecting the items in the chamber. After a moment the man realized Gungren was there and shooed him away.

A lady with an impressive badge stepped up to them.

"Do you have anything to declare?"

They all looked a bit confused, except Winchester—who seemed to be enjoying their flustering. Whizzfiddle sneered as he finished putting his boots back on.

"Well, do you need to declare something?" she repeated.

"We do?"

"Do you?"

"I suppose that depends."

"Look," the guard said, "if you have something to declare, you need to do it now or you'll be thrown out of the Afterlife."

"Hell damn," Zel attempted.

Whizzfiddle hoped the pills would not be effective in the Afterlife and that Zel was just riding a high. He studied the guard and found that she was not the type to put up with mischief. Not that he had planned any. It was just good to know.

"We have nothing to declare," he said strongly.

"Are you certain?" she replied.

He was not.

"It's okay," Orophin said, stepping forward and pulling Whizzfiddle back slightly. "You don't have to protect me."

The elf took a deep breath and faced the guard.

"I'm gay."

CRUMBLING WALLS

Treneth and Ibork arrived at the Monday guild meeting early. The plan was simple, for Treneth. Ibork, however, was about to put everything on the line.

"You will have to be strong, Ibork. Don't let Muppy or Zotrinder intimidate you. Talk powerfully, as is your power."

"Right," Ibork mumbled, looking more afraid than a mouse surrounded by cats.

The two worked for the better part of an hour getting all available wizards via their TalkyThingies. A lot of the wizards had difficulty with the communication device. They could be heard shouting and hitting it with a stick instead of speaking into it, and a couple had seemingly crushed the device outright. Some of the more intellectual understood what was going on and, while assuredly reluctant, agreed to sit in for the day's proceedings.

As a matter of course, all wizards were supposed to attend the council meetings in some fashion at least once a week. Few obliged.

Zotrinder and the Croomplatt twins arrived moments

before the bell. They said their hellos and "ha's" but seemed a bit wary about the unfolding scene.

"What is going on here?" Zotrinder asked.

Ibork looked over at Treneth. Treneth nodded his head in a "go on" gesture.

"I, uh…" Ibork said and then coughed and pulled himself up. "I don't answer to you, Zotrinder."

Zotrinder harrumphed and shook his head. Then he sat down next to Treneth, leaning as far away as possible, and focused his attention on his nails.

Muppy stepped into the room as everything went quiet.

"I trust I'm not late," she said just as the bell rang. "Ah, indeed, I'm right on time."

She skipped up to the podium and pulled forth her gavel, tapping it lightly.

"It is a lovely day today," she said to no one in particular. "Shall we begin?"

Roughly one hundred voices chorused, "We shall."

Muppy froze and then spun on Treneth. She was awfully pale, he thought with a smile, and she suddenly looked intently irritable. Quite a change from the bouncy lady who had skipped up to the podium.

"You," she said, pointing hotly at Treneth. "What is the meaning of this?"

Treneth feigned surprise. "I'm sorry, madam?"

"Why are there all these wizards…attending today?"

"I believe you should ask Ibork that question," Treneth said with his hands up.

"Ibork?"

"I have an announcement to make," Ibork said as confidently as he could.

"Don't act like you don't know what's going on," Muppy hissed as she turned back to Treneth. "We had a deal."

"I'm sorry, madam," Treneth said with his eyebrows raised. "I don't know what you're talking about."

He crossed his legs and rested his gloved hands on a knee. Muppy's eyes were darting around the room. Treneth loved the drama of the moment.

Muppy turned back to Ibork, who was now sweating profusely. He had one eye on the door...and the other one was too.

"Councilman Ibork," Treneth said, "is there something to say or not?"

"*I* run this council, Treneth of Dahl."

Treneth bowed his head. "Of course, madam. My apologies."

"Ibork? What have you got to say?"

Ibork started to get up. He looked a bit wobbly. He waved his hands and sat back down.

"It can wait."

Zotrinder laughed.

"You brought all these wizards into the meeting, many of whom are likely still recovering from a night's sleep, and you are going to make them wait?"

"Ha," the Croomplatt's added, though a little out of sync.

"I do insist, Councilman Ibork," Muppy said, stepping away from the podium. "I relinquish the podium to you for two minutes."

As she sat down, Ibork dragged himself to the podium.

"I, uh…" Ibork started again, speaking much quieter than was normal. "I put in a bid for the chair."

"What?" a hundred voices said and then began chattering.

"I put in a bid for the chair," he said a little louder.

The chattering stopped. Ibork's hands were gripping the podium so tightly that Treneth could see them shaking. Sweat poured off the fat little man. The halfling was only a few months away from a heart attack as it was. The added stress would only serve to expedite matters.

"I'm sorry," Treneth said, almost gleefully, "did you say that you were putting in a bid for the guild chair?"

"That's what he said, Treneth," Muppy responded, "and don't think for a moment that your innocent act is fooling anyone. You're a weasel and everyone here, including the people on the conference, know it."

"I beg your pardon, madam," Treneth said, rising. "I will not tolerate being spoken to in such a manner."

"What is it you will do, Treneth?" She pushed Ibork off the podium and directed him back to his chair. "Are you going to send a shipment of gavels to my house, maybe?"

This time Treneth blanched. Rimpertuz! How could he betray his master's trust like this? And for a woman, no less! Treneth had to think quickly. While Rimpertuz was dumb enough to fall for his manipulations, he was certain that the combined front of Muppy and the rest of the council could indict him quite nicely. He didn't want to spend the rest of his days in jail.

No, he thought, Muppy wouldn't risk it. If she brought charges upon Treneth, her little Rimpertuz would end up convicted as well. The man was Treneth's apprentice, after all. Treneth could easily state that Rimpertuz was completely informed of the entire situation. Who could combat that? Masters often shared with their apprentices so they could grow and learn. Why else would they be apprenticed?

"Treneth," Muppy whispered, covering the speaker on the TalkyThingy, "I know what you're thinking, and you're right. So just sit down, keep your mouth shut, and everyone walks away none the wiser."

Treneth sat, finding an entirely new respect for the councilwoman. He was also pleased she didn't turn evidence on him. It meant she was now an accomplice as well. She was protecting her beau.

"My fellow wizards," Muppy spoke toward the speaker, "are any of you in favor of allowing Councilman Ibork to take over my chair on the guild?"

There was a resounding, "No."

"Excellent," she said. "Now, to be fair, I'm assuming that Councilman Ibork has just cause for chancing such a usurpation. Would you care to share your reasons, Councilman?"

"No, madam," Ibork said meekly.

"I thought you would not," Muppy said. "Ladies and gentleman, I will extend an apology on behalf of Councilman Ibork. Please return to your slumber or toil and I will have the minutes of this meeting delivered to you as is our course."

There were countless "clicks," many proceeded with "ridiculous" and "Ibork." Some combined the terms in one fashion or another. Finally the speaker's light went dim.

"Well done, Treneth," Muppy said, still smiling. "I believe you have successfully damaged Councilman Ibork's reputation in this little power-play."

"I have no idea what you're talking about," Treneth replied.

"I'm sure you haven't," she said.

He said nothing as Muppy flipped open the guild book and started rattling off the day's topics. She seemed quite pleased with herself.

Treneth had underestimated her. Even worse, he had underestimated his apprentice. *Former* apprentice, that is.

As it played right now, Treneth still held the cards. Unless Rimpertuz wanted to go to jail, he would remain silent. Muppy would keep her mouth shut too since she was also now part of this tangled web.

Regardless, both Muppy and Rimpertuz were now as good as dead. Treneth was not one to leave loose ends. Some accident would befall them before the month was out. Of that, Treneth was certain.

"...which concludes the payments for this season on the guild's building rental," Muppy was saying. "That brings us to our next topic."

She tapped her gavel heavily and the door opened. Rimpertuz walked in and stood in the center of the floor.

"What is going on here?" Treneth said, pulling his gloves tightly.

"As to that," Muppy said, running her finger along the page, "it seems that Rimpertuz Niptiwezzle is requesting to be released from his apprenticeship from one Treneth of Dahl."

"What!"

## A FORMER MASTER

*T*he next morning, Whizzfiddle awoke and cast his normal hangover spell to clear his mind. He was a bit shocked that it was required even in the Afterlife.

He had quite enjoyed spending time with Herbie. It had been a few lifetimes since he'd seen his former master and the man hadn't changed one iota. Herbie was still better at partying than he'd ever been with magic.

Reflecting on the previous day, Whizzfiddle was surprised that things had gone so smoothly. He'd expected some opposition from the various trainers, but it seemed they were hungry for a challenge. The Afterlife was a wonderful place for the likes of the lazy, a.k.a. wizards, but those poor souls driven to achieve found it dull at best.

There was a Lady Cliffen, who was a knight of renown in the previous age. She was the first knight recorded to have successfully slain a dragon. The Lady was tasked with aiding Zel.

King Diamondmolar had led the jewel excursion of 675. It was said that the dwarfs were looked down upon until then. They were still looked down upon today because they were vertically challenged, but no longer because of their lack of resources. Bekner was sent off to work with the king, who had exclaimed a plethora of expletives at seeing how tall and hairless Bekner was.

The elves were the most ascended race, but few of them were bored with the Afterlife. It wasn't because they were lazy. On the contrary. It was because they had their forests and animals. It was truly a haven for them. Fortunately, Tunere Lidoos had taken a shine to Orophin. This was not unexpected.

Winchester hadn't bothered to wait for his assignment. He had just hopped on Yultza's shoulder and she sprinted off. Whizzfiddle looked in the direction they were running and saw a mammoth castle in the distance.

That left Gungren. Whizzfiddle had been worried about this part because giants and gorgans were not well known for being the ascendable sort. But there was one of each race that had ascended thus far, and more were expected in the next age to meet the diversity requirements of the Afterlife. Pugz was to help Gungren, and Pugz was a true giant. Dumb as a rock and well-versed at throwing them. Gungren had not wanted to go, but that hadn't bothered Pugz as he carried the kicking little giant away with him.

They were all given two days to do what they could. Whizzfiddle could only hope it would be enough.

Whizzfiddle walked out to the patio. Herbie was resting in a lounge chair that sat under a large blue umbrella. The weather, of course, was flawless.

"You should join us here," his former master said. "Maybe just stay on and send the others back."

It was tempting: the unending relaxation, weather that fit one's own desire, ale that rivaled Gilly's... The list was endless.

Then he thought of real life. This, of course, made him

think of his house. He hoped Sander was keeping everything in line, though he fully expected there would be a fair amount of cleaning to be done upon his return.

And return he must.

There would be time for the Afterlife when his real life was over. He had a sponsor in Herbie to ensure quick acceptance when the time came.

"No," Whizzfiddle said finally. "I have to go back. I gave my word."

"Word schmerd, my former apprentice," Herbie said. "You're here now. They're here now. Enjoy and relax. Eternity is a long time."

"That it is." Whizzfiddle smiled lightly. "Unfortunately, I have only a temporary visa."

He walked to the veranda and set his glass on the rail. The fields were immaculate, just waiting to be explored.

There were no bugs. Well, there were mosquitoes, because vampires were also allowed to ascend. This made little sense to Whizzfiddle since the creatures of the night were essentially eternal beings anyway—unless one got tagged with a decent pesticide. Fortunately, vampires didn't bite here. Their need for blood vanished when gaining entrance, which for them was in and of itself heaven.

"Remember that it will only seem a few years to you before I return for good," Whizzfiddle said.

"That's true, but it will be well over a thousand for you."

Whizzfiddle sighed. "This afternoon I will have to check on the others and prepare to leave."

"Right," Herbie responded. "I can see you'll not be pressured. I'll let it go. I must say that it's been nice having you around again, though."

It wasn't common to have true friendship blossom out of a master-apprentice relationship. Respect, on occasion, but not friendship. There was too much business about the construct of the relationship to allow for it. Before Whizzfiddle was sworn in as a full wizard, the two maintained that professionalism. They kept a strict schedule of partying and tavern-hopping during those times.

"Being here has been the highlight of this quest, my old friend," Whizzfiddle said. "Sadly, tonight I must return."

# A FUTURE SULLIED

*A*s he finished filling one of the barrels with a fresh supply of ostrich feces, Treneth decided he would have to hire someone to help him manage. He thought of Rimpertuz and spat. This was quite telling since Treneth was not the spitting type.

Three weeks and no word about Whizzfiddle, the council was more wary of him than usual, and his apprentice was gone. That things were not going as he had planned was a bit of an understatement.

It was bad enough that Treneth had been given papers by Whizzfiddle so many years ago, but being dismissed as an apprentice wasn't unheard of. Rare, certainly, but it still happened from time to time. Having your apprentice dismiss *you*, though? That *was* unheard of.

He had checked the records and only one case had been found in the last thousand years, and that had been due to the master dying during a quest the two were on. The master ended up as a ghost tied to an ancient burial ground that was in the snowy peaks of Kesper's Range. The apprentice had no interest in spending the rest of his training in the snow with a bunch of ghosts.

But that had been an extreme predicament.

Treneth of Dahl was the first master to be released under normal circumstances. It was not something he wanted to put in his resume.

This happenstance made it more difficult for Treneth to terminate Muppy and Rimpertuz. It would most assuredly fall back on him as being the prime suspect now. All he could do was hope they wouldn't tell anyone about the Pecklesworthy incident. Then he would wait. Once the dust settled and everyone forgot about the situation, Treneth would strike them both down.

With everything else falling apart, Whizzfiddle's demise was the only remaining thing Treneth could hold on to. It was now the focus of his existence, which was frustrating since Treneth had no way of knowing the progress of the old fool.

That would be done soon. Then Treneth would begin plotting the destruction of Rimpertuz and Muppy, and it would be thorough and biting.

"Vigilance," Treneth said to a nearby ostrich. "Vigilance and patience."

The ostrich deposited a fresh batch of magical essence and walked away.

## KNIGHTS AND WIZARDS

hizzfiddle left Herbie's cottage around mid-afternoon in order to gather up the troops.

Time was ticking comfortably in the Afterlife, but in the real world it was flowing faster, and his deadline loomed. Even if all of his charges didn't succeed in changing back to what they were, there was still hope that some would. Maybe, with luck, the council would rule in his favor.

That assumed Treneth hadn't gotten them wrapped up already.

He heard shrieks and bellows as he approached Lady Cliffen's training grounds. The bellowing came from the Lady, the shrieks belonged to Zel.

Zel was in the middle of the field, a sword lying a good ten yards away.

"Now," Lady Cliffen yelled.

"Urk!"

Zel was yelping in a high-pitched voice, covering his face and turning away from the sword each time it landed in front of him. At least the former knight was no longer using expletives.

It was a sad sight to see.

Knights were known to be fearless. They had to be. At a moment's notice, a knight could be thrown into war, tasked with slaying a dragon or, worse, put on traffic-duty during the holidays. Those horse-and-carriage drivers did so tend to pile up if not kept in check.

He approached the two and said his hellos.

"Zel," Whizzfiddle said as he placed his arm on Lady Cliffen's shoulder, "why don't you go grab a drink? A stiff one preferably."

"For you, sir?"

"No, Zel, for you. We will join you momentarily."

"It's no use," she said as they watched Zel go. "The man has no strength, he's afraid of his own shadow, and he refuses to touch a weapon. It's disgusting."

"Remember how he came to be this way, Lady," Whizzfiddle said. "He can't be blamed for this change in his heart. The man's past deeds should be the only consideration here."

Lady Cliffen grunted and retrieved the fallen sword.

"I've never seen the likes of a...knight act like that."

"Magic can be an evil thing," Whizzfiddle said. "You know, there has always been a rift between our two professions. Wizards are known to dislike the viciousness of the soldier's ways. Slicing, stabbing...it's all so grizzly, so barbaric to us."

"And your ways," the Lady said, "are cowardly and, often, too powerfully capable."

"Exactly," Whizzfiddle said, to which the Lady looked a bit shocked. "The reality is that your methods are no more barbaric than ours are cowardly. And our ways"—he motioned toward the departing Zel—"can be rather barbaric indeed."

Whizzfiddle found a nice rock and sat upon it.

"We're really not all that different in how we build our craft. A knight goes through years of training, working with weapons and learning that honor infuses all that you do. A wizard requires study, patience, practice, and concentration. And, in my case, a healthy dose of spirits." And, he left out, a good knowledge of where all the best taverns were in any given land.

"Yes, I suppose."

"The point is that one person's struggle is no less challenging than another's. I'll fully admit that wizarding is more relaxing than soldiering, but our apprenticeships are quite akin, and our methods are often similar. One uses a blade, the other a wand."

Lady Cliffen shrugged. "Where are you going with this?"

"There comes a time when old methods don't work. There comes a time when a soldier needs a wizard and when a wizard needs a soldier."

"That's arguable."

"I needed you to help me with Zel, did I not?"

"True," she said, "but it's proving fruitless."

Whizzfiddle smiled. "That's because you need me too."

"Fine," she replied after a few deep breaths. "What did you have in mind?"

It took a fair amount of booze to create the scene, but within minutes there was a marching of horses and a few carriages. It was no royal parade, but it was passable as an envoy. There was only so much one wizard could pull off without getting completely blitzed out of his mind.

A trumpet sounded. Whizzfiddle winked at Lady Cliffen as Zel burst out of the house. He looked a little bedazzled as he came running down the hill.

"What is happening?"

"The queen arrives for her normal inspection," Lady Cliffen said.

"What? Here?"

"Is it not her right to inspect all troops, past and future? We are still at her beck and call, are we not?"

Zel looked ready to answer but he merely frowned.

"There!" Whizzfiddle pointed to the top of a large hill, and then he fell over.

A group of mounted horses crested the area. They blew their battle horn and began trampling down the hill. The queen's knights turned to the advancing band of ruffians as her chariot picked up its pace away from the coming battle.

"Oh no," Zel shrieked. "They'll be overrun."

"Is there anything you can do?" Lady Cliffen said to Whizzfiddle as she hauled him back to his feet.

"I'm not sure of my juris...juri..." He hiccupped. "Juris...diction in the Afterlife."

"Does that matter now?" Zel asked. "The Queen is in dire need, man!"

Zel bolted toward the training grounds without looking back. Lady Cliffen turned and bowed to Whizzfiddle. He winked in return.

Within moments, Knight Zelbaldian Riddenhaur galloped out of the gates on a battle steed. He had on a helm and shield and he was carrying a shining sword. But the field was empty. The scene had died away.

"What is this trickery?" Zel exclaimed in a voice that was powerful and confident.

Then it must have hit him what had really happened. He trotted over, laughing heartily. He jumped from the horse and slammed the blade into the ground with a swift motion, and then removed his helm.

"It seems I owe you both a great debt."

"Seeing a knight returned to his true form is payment enough for me," Lady Cliffen replied with a smile.

"Preparing yourself for the return back will do nicely for

my part," Whizzfiddle said as he started to depart, casting a sobering spell and doing his best to walk a straight line. "I knew you had it in you, Sir Rid...Rid—"

"Riddenhaur," Zel said.

"That's the one," he called over his shoulder. "See you tonight."

## SHORT AGAIN

*D*iamondmollar and Bekner were nowhere to be found at the king's hovel.

Whizzfiddle looked about, one cave after another, following the twists and turns that always led him back to the entrance. Each section had piles of jewels and diamonds strewn about on the smooth floors. There were roughly twenty such caves, but the day was moving on so he determined to come back after checking on the others.

*Ding.*

"I know that sound," Whizzfiddle said.

Whizzfiddle moved from cave mouth to cave mouth, seeking out the source of the dwarf's hammer.

He found the source and entered, noting there were cheers surrounding each slam of the hammer. Maybe Diamondmollar was showing Bekner a motivational film.

A large framed piece of glass ran the length of a flat wall near the back of the third tunnel. Through the portal, Whizzfiddle saw a mass of dwarfs rallying around Bekner. The large dwarf was wielding a hammer that dwarfed the nearest, well, dwarf, and he was slamming it on a rock face of the largest wall of diamond Whizzfiddle had ever seen. After each smack on the wall, Bekner would then crack an anvil, hence that proverbial *ding* that had caught Whizzfiddle's attention.

*Brilliant*, Whizzfiddle thought with a smile.

King Diamondmollar had been the leader of the Diamond Tunnelers clan before he had ascended. He was responsible for more jewel-collecting expeditions than any in the clan's history, but there was one rock face that they were never able to penetrate. Diamondmollar had named it "The Glittering Fortress" because, as he put it, it "was after being glittery and the damnable thing was as impenetrable as a fortress." The dwarfs had estimated there to be more value in a single wall of the fortress than in the combination of all their findings in history, and they had set about on numerous quests, both individually and as teams, to try and conquer it. None had even come close. Most returned sore, battered, and dejected, losing all confidence in their dwarven ability, and not a single hammer had ever stayed intact.

The night the king left the world, he made a prophecy that one day a dwarf of extraordinary capability would rise above all others and break into the fortress.

*Ding. Crack.*

"Interesting," Whizzfiddle said as a hairline crack appeared in the wall.

*Ding. Crack. Ding! Crack!*

Support was rampant now as the wall was splintering. Shards of diamond were dropping off like a melting iceberg.

"Get in here with yer hammers flying, ya mangy bunch," King Diamondmollar yelled about the din.

A swarm of hammer-slinging dwarfs pounded the wall that Bekner had broken through. For every hundred mini-thwacks there was a resounding one from the hammer of the lofty dwarf. It didn't take long before there was a gap large enough for a dwarf to enter the glittering fortress.

As soon as the wall collapsed, a twinkling of light surrounded Bekner. He yelped and dropped to the ground, nearly crushing a number of dwarfs on the way down.

Everyone dropped their hammers to come to his aid.

Whizzfiddle couldn't see through all the ruddy helms and beards until, as one, they all gasped and backed away.

Bekner was glowing and the light was getting brighter. The giant dwarf groaned and then yelled out as a flash consumed the scene, blinding everyone momentarily, including Whizzfiddle.

He waited for his eyes to readjust and then looked back.

"I'll be damned," Whizzfiddle said. "The dwarf is...half again."

Whizzfiddle stepped through the window and out into the midst of applauds. He pushed his way through to Bekner and knelt down to have a look at him. The dwarf's beard was back, thick and knotted as any respectable dwarf's would be.

"You looked better taller," the wizard said with a wink.

"Aye," Bekner said, "and you humans were after smelling better when my nose was a fair bit above your asses."

They shared a laugh as King Diamondmollar stepped in.

"Proud dwarfs," the king said, "the prophecy has been fulfilled. Long shall the name Bekner *Diamondcrusher* live!"

A hearty surge of rejoicing ensued as Whizzfiddle helped the dwarf to his feet. Diamondmollar grabbed Bekner by the shoulder and moved him to the entrance of the fortress.

"You'll be the first in, lad," the king said. "You've earned it."

"Bekner," Whizzfiddle said, "I shall await you back in the Afterlife when you're done here. Please don't, um, celebrate too much, as we have a timetable to keep."

"Aye," Bekner said. "I pay my debts, wizard. And I'm after owing you a rather large one."

## PRETTY AGAIN

*T*he forests were lush and peaceful. Birdsong flowed in harmony as Whizzfiddle walked toward the home of Tunere Lidoos, snapping twigs with each step. The fresh smell of flowers floated along the breeze and gave the elderly wizard a sense of calm.

The elves had it right.

"You're encroaching on private property, friend," a voice said from behind him.

He put up his hands and slowly turned to face a flawless elf. The elf smiled at him.

"It can't be."

"It is," Orophin said, leaping lithely forward and embracing the wizard.

Whizzfiddle was overjoyed for the lad and patted him heartily on the back. Then he abruptly stepped back.

"It's not me, is it?" Whizzfiddle said, rising an eyebrow.

Orophin grimaced momentarily, and then they both laughed.

"I'm so happy for you, lad," Whizzfiddle said as they moved off to meet with Tunere.

Whizzfiddle explained what had happened with Zel and Bekner, which seemed to greatly please Orophin. It was clear that the troop had grown close through their shared ordeal. They were irrevocably connected now. Trials had a way of sewing binds, even amongst those who would otherwise loathe each other's company.

The three shared a small meal and Orophin told Whizzfiddle how he had gotten his illustrious self back.

"His problem," Tunere said, "was that he had forgotten what it meant to be an elf."

"Arrogance?"

"The love of nature and natural things," Orophin replied.

"But—"

"So," Tunere interrupted before Whizzfiddle could finish his comment, "I set in place a situation where one of my does was in need of aid."

Whizzfiddle was surprised. "You purposefully injured a deer?"

"Of course not," Tunere responded heatedly. "What kind of elf would I be had I done that?"

"My apologies."

"I simply allowed nature to take its course."

Whizzfiddle raised an eyebrow.

Tunere sighed. "I threw a stick and the deer chased it, tripped over a stack of logs and cut its leg."

"They chase sticks?"

"Ours do," Tunere said. "Anyway, the poor thing had a gashing wound."

"When I saw the fallen doe," Orophin jumped in, "I felt my blood flow. Its eyes were in a state of terror."

The elf paused and took a deep breath.

"That little deer brought me back to who I was. She saved me."

The elf pointed at the field where a deer was hopping and playing amongst the lilies.

"It wasn't until I had her wound cleaned and patched that I noticed I had returned to my former self."

They finished their meal and Whizzfiddle said his goodbyes, reminding Orophin of the timetable.

## PLAYING WITH ROCKS

The place that Pugz called home was exactly where you would expect a giant to live. It was sparse, unappealing, and covered with boulders. The only redeeming quality Whizzfiddle could make out was a lone tree that sat in the middle of the field. No doubt this served as Pugz's lavatory.

"You throw rock now," Pugz hollered as Whizzfiddle rounded the corner of the giant's den.

Gungren was too short to peer over the "rock" that Pugz was pointing at, much less lift it. Instead, Gungren was sitting and reading one of his books.

"How are things moving along?" Whizzfiddle said.

Gungren scrambled to his feet, stuffing the book into his pack and adjusting his hat. Then he picked up his staff and headed toward Whizzfiddle and Pugz.

"He no throw rock," said Pugz.

"We go now?" Gungren said.

Whizzfiddle frowned.

"Gungren, you are not keeping up your end of the bargain."

"I in Afterlife," Gungren said. "I not say I do more than that."

Whizzfiddle thought back. Damn. Gungren was going to make a good wizard someday.

"Well," Whizzfiddle said. "I'm amending the deal, then."

"You can't do that."

"I just did, little man. Either you accept the training as given, or you'll not be my apprentice."

"That not fair."

"Many things in life aren't fair, Gungren."

Gungren threw down his bag and approached the boulder. It wouldn't even budge. He grunted and pushed until his feet slid out from under him, making tracks in the dirt.

"Maybe a smaller one to start, eh Pugz?"

"Yeah, that good plan." Pugz pointed to another. "You throw that one."

Gungren pulled himself up and brushed off his robe. He strode over to the next rock and was able to launch it a good three feet. Then he dropped into the dirt, looking exhausted.

"That it?" Pugz said. "You no giant! You an embr...embared—"

"Embarrassment," Whizzfiddle aided.

"That the one," Pugz said, pointing at Whizzfiddle.

The fact was, a giant only did giant-like things when it was angry. Just having him pick up a rock and throw it wouldn't do much. Gungren had to get truly angry.

"I guess that's that, then," Whizzfiddle said. "You tried, Gungren. Sort of."

"Good," Gungren said. "We go now?"

"I'm afraid not," Whizzfiddle said. "I can't take on an apprentice with such a low work ethic."

"*You* lazy," Gungren said in shock. "You say all wizards is lazy!"

"True, true," Whizzfiddle replied, "but I had to earn my right to be lazy. There was a time when I had to"—he shuddered—"work very hard. I toiled for my master as he taught me the wizard's way, and many apprentices toil incessantly in search of their power source. I was one of the lucky ones, yes, but you may not be."

"What you mean?"

"You don't know your essence yet, Gungren. It could take you a hundred years to find out where you get your power. You may even die before you ever learn what it is." He squatted down and placed a hand on the little giant's shoulder. "That means you will be my apprentice until the day you die, if you don't find your source, and that means you'll never once, in all that time, cast a single spell."

"I could find it sooner," Gungren said sternly. "I work hard to find."

Whizzfiddle laughed and rose back up.

"Hard to believe that you'll work hard when you give up in the face of opposition right here, my dinky buddy." He turned to Pugz. "Sorry, Pugz, I had great hopes for this one."

"I didn't."

"No? Well, you tried your best."

"Not really."

"Hmmm." Whizzfiddle scratched his beard and then shrugged. "Oh well. Good luck to you, Gungren. I'm sure someone will send you back to town at some point, seeing that you do have potential."

"What? You gonna leave me here?"

"He say you stay," Pugz said, knocking Gungren on his butt. "Then you stay."

Gungren got up and charged at the giant, hitting him hard in the shin. To Whizzfiddle's surprise, Pugz howled in agony. It seemed that giants knew where the soft spots were on other giants. This didn't go over very well with Pugz, though. The real giant picked up the tiny one and launched him like he would a small rock.

Whizzfiddle cringed as he watched Gungren zoom through the air in a very high arc.

After what seemed an eternity, the tiny giant landed with a *poof* on a huge mound of soft dirt. Everything went quiet, aside from Pugz rubbing his shin and whimpering. Then a figure stirred in the dust.

Gungren was alive, in an Afterlife-manner-of-speaking.

As the dust cleared, Whizzfiddle noted that Gungren had a mouthful of dirt and a boulder easily twice his size resting neatly over his head. This was odd since there were no boulders over where the dunes were. With a grunt, the rock flew from Gungren's hands, a bit of light trailing in its wake, and it was heading directly toward Pugz.

*Thump*, the rock seemed to say as it met Pugz's massive noggin.

Pugz groaned and then fell over. It didn't knock him out, per se, but he looked a bit dazed. Whizzfiddle made a mental note that a head shot to a giant was not as effective as a nice rap to the shin.

A blink later, Gungren was standing right next to him, looking angry.

"How did you..." Whizzfiddle started and then stopped. "The dirt!"

"Whuh?" Gungren said, spitting.

"It's the dirt, Gungren. You've found your essence already!"

"I dithd," Gungren mumbled as he drooled dirt.

"Ha!" Whizzfiddle answered in Croomplattian fashion. "I fear there is more to you than is clear yet, but I also fear you're not going to be turning back into a proper giant anytime soon."

Pugz raised his head. He looked at Gungren and smiled.

"You pass," he said and then the lights went out.

"Now we go?"

Whizzfiddle shrugged.

"I suppose we've no other option, my young...*apprentice.*" Gungren's grin was as big as Pugz's had been. "We have a timetable to keep."

"What about him?" Gungren said.

"He'll be fine," Whizzfiddle said. "You of all people should know what a giant's head can withstand. And we're in the Afterlife, so it's not like he could die any further than he already has. Besides,"—he glanced at the cracked rock—"it looks like the boulder took the dragon's share of the damage."

## TAMING OF A DRAGON

*Y*ultza was standing at the dragon's pass when Whizzfiddle and Gungren arrived. She stepped in the way of the gate as they approached.

Whizzfiddle looked over the castle and its grounds. It was enormous. No, enormous was too small a word to describe the place. Even a gorgan would feel dwarfed here. The top of the castle's snow-tipped points disappeared into the clouds. Only in the Afterlife could such a structure even exist.

*Dragons*, he thought with a shake of his head.

"Good afternoon, Yultza," Whizzfiddle said. "We are here to see Winchester."

"He is busy at this time," she replied firmly.

"That's all and well, but we have a time—"

"You will need to wait," Yultza said, crossing her arms.

Gungren walked up to her and lifted her off the ground and moved her into the grass. She slammed fist after fist at the back of his head, but only accomplished bruising her hands. *He might come in handy after all*, thought Whizzfiddle.

"Don't worry," Whizzfiddle said to her. "I'll only be a moment."

Dragons were known for their massive jewel- and gold-filled caves. Many slept on their hoard for years, luxuriating in the gleam of treasures they could never actually spend, even if they had the gumption. But there were no jewels as far as Whizzfiddle could see. He assumed they were hidden in some underground labyrinth.

"Hello?" he called out.

There was no response. He tried again a few times, raising his voice magically with each attempt.

"Whizzfiddle?" Winchester said, peeking out from a room at the top of the stairs.

"Unless you know of some other elderly wizard..." He stopped and remembered that the Afterlife was full of geriatric sorcerers. "Yes, it's me."

"Time to go already, then?" Winchester said.

"Just about. You know how time moves more quickly in the real world."

"Valid," Winchester said.

"Come back, lover," a booming voice said from behind Winchester.

Try as he might, Whizzfiddle could not see into the room and he wasn't about to climb all those stairs.

"I'll be back shortly, my dear," Winchester called over his shoulder. "You just rest up until I return, yes?"

Winchester adjusted his little red velvet robe and pulled out a pipe. He patted his jacket for a match and shrugged, slipping the pipe back in place.

"I do apologize for the interruption," Whizzfiddle said. "I had not expected you two would be, well, compatible."

Winchester laughed and leaned on one of the banister rails.

"I have my ways of pleasing the ladies," he said.

Whizzfiddle had little choice other than to be impressed.

How a lizard could tame a full-sized dragon was baffling. Whizzfiddle tipped his proverbial hat to the small creature.

Small creature?

"Wait," Whizzfiddle said. "You didn't change back?"

"Obviously," Winchester replied. "I did so try, but my mind wouldn't budge."

Whizzfiddle's shoulders sagged. With both Winchester and Gungren not being returned to their normal stature, Whizzfiddle's chances at winning this case was nil.

"I see," Whizzfiddle said finally. "I would have assumed that your, um, equipment would have come up, well…short, and that would have made you want to return to your dragon status."

"You humans are so entrapped by size-envy. After a thousand years of life yourself, even you should know that size doesn't matter."

"Not as much as being perpetually in my six-hundreds does, true."

"There you go," Winchester said smugly.

"Bring back the camera, lover," came the dragon's voice again. "I haven't felt this sexy in a long time!"

"Ah-hah!" Whizzfiddle laughed. "You're merely taking pictures of her!"

Winchester slumped and began tapping the rail.

"I would imagine she's, what…" Whizzfiddle said, "one hundred feet long, or more? And with you not even a foot long, it's not difficult to do the math. I mean, it's not like you vibrate or anything. Or do you?"

Winchester just crossed his arms.

"It's all making sense now," Whizzfiddle said while leaning on his walking staff.

"What's making sense?"

"Why you came along with us. You didn't care about the

rest of the troop. You just needed pictures of a dragon for your silly magazine."

"That's not true. I have grown rather fond of a few of them and so I genuinely wanted to help. And why does everyone keep calling it a silly magazine? It's not silly. Dirty, sure. Silly? Never. Well, maybe if I put a jokes section in or something." The lizard paused. "Actually, that's not a bad idea."

"What would you have done had we not come to the Afterlife? It's not like there are dragons all over the place..." Whizzfiddle stopped and looked up at Winchester. "Oh no, you wouldn't have!"

Winchester shrugged. "It doesn't matter now."

"Yeah, but Isis? Even you can't think she's attractive."

"I needed a dragon. It's a stretch, sure, but she's close enough."

Whizzfiddle had only seen Isis once. Her full name was Isickly Kandoop and she lived in a cave deep in the woods of Kek. The poor thing was the meekest dragon he had ever met. She had one eye, a missing front leg, a full row of non-pointy teeth—which made her a herbivore, a set of wings so small that she was incapable of flying, and she couldn't breathe fire. Actually, her breath was rather minty. On top of all this, she was so sweet that not a single knight ever raised a sword against her even when sent to do so.

"Now," Winchester said, "if you'll leave me alone with my dear Zudania for, say, another hour or so, I'll keep my word to you and will meet you at the gate. I do have a magazine to publish, you know?"

Whizzfiddle looked up in shock. Zudania?

Zudania Pontzontonia was the longest-living dragon in the known histories of Ononokin. She had defeated scores of knights and soldiers of fortune. It was only after her ten-thousandth year that she accepted a slot in the Afterlife. It was said that she was secure in that no other dragon would break her survival record any time soon.

Having her picture in *PlayDragon* would sell thousands of copies on legend alone.

"We leave tonight, Winchester."

"I'll be there."

# THE HOMECOMING

*T*he days were running together for Treneth.

All his plans were falling apart, the guild seemed stronger because of him but more in an in-spite-of-him sort of way. His ruse had done little more than strengthen their binds against him. They had even accepted Ibork back into their fold.

Worse, Treneth had taken a sudden liking for wine. After a long day's toil in the ostrich field, Treneth had found he needed some way to relax. It turned out that wine was good for that.

It was in his DNA. His father was quite renowned for his drinking prowess.

He was on his fifth glass when someone knocked at his door.

"Rimpertuz?" he said as his former apprentice stood before him. "You've come back?"

"Mistress Muppy sent me to fetch you, sir," he said. "Master Whizzfiddle and his questing crew has returned and they are about to hold session."

Treneth instantly sobered as his glass dropped to the floor.

# A CASE PRESENTED

*W*hizzfiddle was finishing up his telling of the wonders he had seen in the Afterlife when Treneth burst through the door shouting that he had arrived. Whizzfiddle raised an eyebrow at how disheveled Treneth looked.

"Why was I not told we were having a council meeting?" Treneth demanded.

"I believe you were summoned," Muppy said, patting the chair next to her where Rimpertuz sat. "Were you not?"

"Well, yes," Treneth replied. "I, uh—"

"Please move to the prosecutor's chair, Treneth," Muppy said. "We would like to get on with this…"—she shook her head—"…trial."

Whizzfiddle found the scene somewhat bittersweet. He had learned of Treneth's attempt at a power-play with the council and could now see what it had done to the man. Inside he wanted to feel happy that Treneth was getting his just reward, but he just couldn't do it. Deserved or not, Treneth was still his former apprentice.

"What's with the orc and the lizard?" Treneth asked.

"As to that," Whizzfiddle replied, "the lizard is a former dragon who was changed along with the rest of the group."

"Ah," Treneth replied. "He seems to still be a lizard to me, unless dragons now offer a smaller variety. This case appears closed."

"Sorry, Treneth," Whizzfiddle answered, scratching his beard, "the fact is that he was not one of the signers of the document."

Treneth fumbled through the papers. "He is…?"

"I am Winchester Hargrath Junior the third."

"The third?" Zotrinder said.

"I believe he said he was 'junior the third,'" Ibork corrected.

Winchester stood a little taller, possibly a quarter of an inch. His name clearly preceded him. After what Whizzfiddle witnessed with Zudania, his own respect for the lizard had doubled.

"And the orc?" Treneth said.

"Also irrelevant," Whizzfiddle said. "No offense, dear," he added quickly. "Her name is Yultza and she is a, um, well—"

"I'm a fashion model," Yultza said.

"Oh?" Muppy said, scooting to the edge of her chair. "What fashions?"

"Skin," Yultza replied.

Treneth slammed the papers on the desk. "Then why are they here?"

"Moral support, mostly," Whizzfiddle said.

"And character testimony," Winchester added.

Treneth laughed at this answer. He walked to the bench and went to place his hands on the rail but withdrew them carefully. The council members seemed relieved.

"We're going to take the word of an orc and a...*dragon* on the wholesomeness of Whizzfiddle's character?"

Yultza stepped forward, but Zel pulled her back.

"Pardon me, sir" Zel said. Everyone eyed him dubiously. "I have served alongside this dragon in battle and have seen him overcome being the most dangerous beast in the realm to being one of the smallest. Yet he still survives. Sully his name or reputation before me again and I, Sir Zelbedain Riddenhaur of Her Majesty's Guard, will be forced to challenge you to a duel."

Treneth was suddenly very pale.

"As you can see," Whizzfiddle spoke out of the side of his mouth, adding a wink, "the knight is back to his old self."

"As am I." Orophin moved to stand next to Zel.

"Aye," Bekner said. "Me too, and it's thanks to this wizard."

Treneth seemed defeated as he went back to his chair. He pulled out the papers again and studied them. Whizzfiddle waited, holding his breath.

"Well, well, well," Treneth said, the gleam coming back into his eye. "I see a knight, an elf, and a dwarf." He looked up over them all. "I see no giant."

"I are here," Gungren said.

Everyone looked down.

"I *am* here," Whizzfiddle corrected.

"I know you am. I can see you." He turned to Orophin. "I think him getting too old."

Treneth marched back up to the council bench and slammed his hands on the rail. They all reared back in horror. Treneth laughed maniacally.

"He *did not* succeed!"

"No," Whizzfiddle said, "technically, I did not."

Gungren tugged his sleeve and pointed at the copy of the contract. Whizzfiddle handed his copy of the contract to Gungren, wondering what his latest apprentice had in mind.

"Thank you," Treneth said to Whizzfiddle. "The law is the law, madam."

"My master done what the contract say to do," said Gungren.

Treneth scoffed. "We don't need to listen to this. Surely the council knows the proper steps to take from here... Wait, did you just call him 'master'?"

"I'll allow it," Muppy said.

"Madam, you can't seriously—"

Muppy stood up, gavel in hand. "I said that I will allow it."

"Fine," Treneth nearly spat. Then he turned back toward Gungren. "How is it, my three-foot friend, that our *esteemed* colleague has completed this quest to the letter of the contract?"

"Four," Gungren said.

"Hmmm?"

"Four feet, not three like you said. He done it because when you messed up first contract, I fixed second one to say specially what it does." Gungren grinned. "See, you not as good with details as you think."

"Is that so?"

"You want me read it?"

Treneth threw his arms in a wide circle. "By all means!"

"Okay," Gungren said and then cleared his throat. "It say, 'Whizzfiddle will, one: help Orophin Telemnar transform back into an elf; two: help Zelbadain Riddenhaur transform back into a knight; three: help Bekner Axehammer transform back into a dwarf; and four: help Gungren transform back into a giant.'"

"I'm now Bekner Diamondcrusher, by the way." The dwarf was obviously highly pleased with his new name.

Treneth clapped his hands in mock applause. He then turned to the council.

"I admit that I find it interesting that a giant—I mean, *former giant*—can read, but that does not mean the contract is fulfilled."

"It was fulfilled when we got to Kek, dumb man," Gungren said.

"Huh?" everyone replied. Okay, everyone but the Croomplatt twins, who hadn't quite gotten the hang of "huh" just yet, but they were close.

"The contract don't say Master Whizzfiddle *will* get us back to what we was. It say that he will *help* get us back to what we was."

Whizzfiddle got it. His new apprentice was cunning indeed! He patted Gungren on the back heartily. This one would be a pleasure to teach, he thought…and learn from, he added to his thought.

The others gathered around Gungren as well.

"That's trivial," Treneth shrieked. "You can't possibly allow that to be admissible, madam."

"In your own words, Treneth," Muppy said, "he must finish it to the *letter* of the contract. And, it appears, to the letter…he has." She slammed her gavel on the podium. "I hereby move that this trial be marked as over and that Whizzfiddle be cleared of all charges. What say you, council?"

"Agreed," Ibork shouted.

"Whatever," Zotrinder said, picking at his cuticles.

"Ha!"

"No!" Treneth said and pulled his gloves off. "I cannot allow this!"

Muppy jumped the rail as if she were in her early twenties. She had her gavel in hand, but Treneth was the quicker. He said a quick incantation and Muppy sank to the ground, looking dazed. Rimpertuz yelled and charged, but he too was no match for Treneth and he hit the ground also. Before the Croomplatts, Ibork, or Zotrinder could get their sources in place, Treneth cast a spell of binding on them.

Whizzfiddle reached into his robe.

"No, no, no," Treneth said, turning on him. "Get your hand out of the robe, old man. You have ruined the better part of my adult life, *Master* Whizzfiddle."

"We've been through this before, Treneth—"

"Silence!"

Whizzfiddle complied. His former apprentice did look a bit crazed and he probably had a full stuffing of ostrich remnants under his nails.

"I will have my satisfaction one way or the other," Treneth said. "I will also finally learn what lies under that damnable hat of yours."

"Is that what this is all about?" Whizzfiddle said.

"Of course not, you old goat. It's about vengeance, but not knowing what the big secret is about what's under your hat has been driving me crazy for years."

"Looks like you've finally arrived, then."

"Silence, I said!"

"Sir," Zel spoke with the voice of authority, "I command that you cease this venture at once."

"Or what?"

Zel withdrew his sword. "Or you will have to contend with my blade."

"And my bow," Orophin added, stringing an arrow.

"And my axe," Bekner said.

"Why does this sound so familiar?" Whizzfiddle whispered.

Treneth merely waved his hand and all three weapons disappeared. It was to be expected. You just couldn't defeat magic with threats. You had to do, not talk about doing.

"Amp phmy pmagiph," something said behind Whizzfiddle.

They all looked back questioningly.

"I phaid," Gungren said, his mouth full of the floor's dirt, "amp phmy pmagiph."

"I believe he said his mapsquid," Zotrinder mumbled as loudly as he could.

"No," Ibork mumbled back. "It sounded like fly sadkid."

"That doesn't even make any sense."

"Oh, but 'mapsquid' does, yes?"

"Ha," the Croomplatt's mumbled.

Gungren looked at Whizzfiddle and winked. The wizard knew what he was up to and so he turned back to Treneth and shrugged, moving enough to block his apprentice from direct view. He slowly lifted his hat.

"That's it?" Treneth said. "Mood hair?"

"It may not be a big deal to you, Treneth, but to someone of my stature, it's a big deal indeed."

"Unbelievable," Treneth said. "I can't believe I let that... You know what? Never mind. Let you and your mood hair be damned. I'm done with you, old man. It's time we finish this."

"I *do* agree, my dear Treneth," Whizzfiddle said as the breeze of a small boulder passed overhead.

Everyone who wasn't frozen ducked. Everyone else's eyes followed the trajectory of the zooming rock. Treneth threw up his hands in an attempt to ward off the impending doom.

*Thump.*

Whizzfiddle felt a mixture of elation and sorrow as Treneth hit the floor. Former apprentice or not, Whizzfiddle had never wished the man ill will. Not serious ill will, anyway. But a boulder launched from the likes of Gungren was ill indeed.

Whizzfiddle resolved to drink an ale in the man's honor.

"I guess that ends that," Muppy said as Treneth's magic lifted from her.

"Is he dead?" Ibork asked.

"Him not dead," Gungren answered. "Him just got knocked out."

Treneth groaned.

"Oh," Whizzfiddle said with relief.

He then resolved to drink an ale in Gungren's honor instead. One way or the other, he was determined to drink some ale.

# THE CELEBRATION

*A*fter the trial had ended and Treneth had been taken away, everyone decided to head off to Whizzfiddle's favorite tavern. This was an unprecedented event as the wizards generally avoided Gilly's like the plague.

Whizzfiddle had to admit he was impressed with how Gungren had dropped a mostly hollowed out boulder on Treneth's head. The rock had been just solid enough to knock him out so the council could magically bind him until authorities arrived.

"He'll be in prison for a good while," Muppy said. "We'll make sure there are no ostriches within eyesight of that pesky weasel, too."

"What about his nails?" Whizzfiddle asked. "He used to be able to pack enough dung under them to last a week."

"Already taken care of," Muppy said. "Zotrinder cast a spell that blasted water and soap all over Treneth's hands until they were clean enough to eat off. Not that I'd recommend it."

"May The Twelve forbid it," Whizzfiddle agreed.

"Zotrinder then went about giving him a nice, tight manicure."

"Impressive," Whizzfiddle said with a nod to Zotrinder.

"I wore gloves, just in case."

"Understandable."

"Yes," Muppy said as Rimpertuz handed her a fresh mug of ale. "It turns out that Treneth had been quite busy over the last few months. After he regained consciousness, he admitted to all sorts of wrongdoings, including his involvement with the pea pod shipment that went to Kek, and also to the fact that he'd used an elixir on me the night that we had dinner together."

"You had dinner with him?" said Whizzfiddle in shock.

"It's complicated," she replied. "However, it *did* lead me to a newfound relationship with my dear Rimpertuz."

"Well, that's nice, at least."

"Anyway," she said after taking a sip of the ale, "now our dear Treneth is sharing a cell with that thief Jetherby."

"Curlang Jetherby?"

"Yes, that's right, and I have to say that Jetherby seemed quite pleased to have a new cellmate."

Whizzfiddle searched his memory. If he recalled correctly, Jetherby was once the king of thieves in the Underworld. Well, "queen" of thieves was more apropos. It was rather strange that he was doing business up in Rangmoon. To be fair, though, it was rather strange that Whizzfiddle had just come back from doing business in the Afterlife. Regardless, Treneth was probably going to learn a thing or two about himself during his prison stay.

Whizzfiddle shrugged and walked over to Orophin, Zel, Bekner, and Winchester.

"My good elf," Whizzfiddle said, "I believe you have a mystery to clear up for us, now that this questing business is all done."

"Do I?"

"Aye, lady...er, laddie," Bekner said. "Who is it?"

"I don't think I want to know," Zel said.

"Me neither," Gungren agreed.

"Gungren, you must always embrace an air of curiosity—"

"I like lady giants."

"No, not your curiosity about..." Whizzfiddle started. "Look, I meant you need to be curious about mysteries!"

"Oh, that okay, then."

"I, for one, have my money on it being Zel," Whizzfiddle said.

"I told you before that it wasn't the knight," Orophin said and then turned to Zel. "No offense."

"None taken," Zel said, looking relieved.

"Well then?"

"It was Winchester," Orophin declared.

"Interesting."

"I knew it all along," the lizard said with a smile. "Face it, people, I'm irresistible. Sadly, I'm also a lady's lizard. Sorry, Orophin."

"It's okay," the elf replied. "Like I said, it *was* you. I think now I will seek out one of my own kind."

"Gay?" Bekner said.

"Of course someone gay, Bekner. What I meant, though, was that I would search for another elf."

"Should be easy to find a gay elf," said Bekner.

"I would imagine a real challenge would be to find a straight one," Zel replied.

"It's probably a wise move," Winchester piped up before Orophin could start his arguments. "Obviously humans and dwarfs are too insensitive to consider as viable partners."

"My thoughts exactly," Orophin responded.

"If you're willing, I could use your help for my next publication."

"Really?"

"Yes, it will be a fellow-to-fellow magazine. I'm planning to call it *PlayElf.*"

The partying went on until the wee hours, but eventually all good things must end. Everyone had to get back to their lives, their people, and in the case of Winchester and Yultza, *PlayDragon.*

By the time Whizzfiddle and Gungren had arrived at the house, it was nearly morning.

The elderly wizard couldn't believe his eyes. The grounds on his property looked immaculate. The siding of his fine abode shone like it hadn't in years.

Sander was out giving orders to a group that appeared barely awake.

"Sander," Whizzfiddle said, "I don't know what to say."

"Praise The Twelve that you're back, sir!"

"The place looks amazing. I'm almost sad to have returned."

Sander called out to everyone. One by one the group of beggars stumbled out of the shed. Each of them appeared haggard and exhausted.

"We're glad you've returned home," Sander said. "We all talked about it a week ago. It was nice to have the baths and the food, but this daily toil is dreadful."

Whizzfiddle understood that.

"You're back," Sander continued, "and we're done. Let's go, boys!"

"And girls," a few of the lasses said without much fuss.

## THE DELIVERY

*T*wo months went by and things were ticking again at the slow pace afforded to a wizard's life.

Gungren was making nice progress on his magic and was not above doing cooking and cleaning when it was warranted. Mostly, though, Whizzfiddle was teaching the tiny giant how to relax, play cards, and throw a few back. Of all the apprentices Whizzfiddle had carried over his years, the little giant was shaping up to be the best.

"Master," Gungren said as he walked into the living room where Whizzfiddle had his feet up, "you got a delivered thing."

"Delivery," Whizzfiddle said.

"Yep, that the one."

Whizzfiddle took the package and carefully opened it. Then he slowly whistled. He was holding issue #1 of *PlayDragon*, which contained Yultza on the cover in a scantily-clad outfit, and she looked rather enticing.

"She look good," Gungren said, "even for an orc."

"One moment," Whizzfiddle said, holding up a finger.

"Wrong one again," Gungren said as he adjusted Whizzfiddle's hand slightly.

"Thank you."

"Yep. I say that Yultza look good in magerthing."

"Magazine."

"That what I said."

Whizzfiddle went to open the magazine when a fold-out picture dropped loose. His eyes widened substantially as his mood hair took on a greenish hue. It was a picture of Yultza in the nude.

Gungren tried to whistle this time. Mostly, he just spit.

"I do agree, Gungren." Whizzfiddle took a sip from his flask as his hair turned a dark shade of green. "I rather do agree."

## A LETTER FROM PEAPOD
## PECKLESWORTHY

*D*ear Reader,

It has been a number of years since I lost my mind in the quaint town of Kek. If it weren't for my lovely wife, Glinayeth Noosebaum-Pecklesworthy, whom I married after my mind returned, I would probably be fumbling about in a field somewhere.

But there is one who is owed a greater deal of gratitude than even my wife. She is one who lives outside of our wonderful land of Ononokin.

I have been given only wisps of the full tale, but from what I've been told she fought against the world's creators for my right to live. Had she not stood her ground, I would have been shot by the guards in the city of Kek.

I have been told her name is Lorelei.

While I have since lobbied that she be allowed to join the ranks of The Twelve, thus making it The Thirteen, the creators have denied my request stating that there is no race of editors available for her to rule over. I have no knowledge if, by editors, they mean those who look over texts, complain a lot, and send constant notes with corrections as they roll their eyes in that holier-than-thou way. If that's what my savior is, then I suppose I must do what I can to treat their lot better.

With no recourse in my stead, I hope that they at least see fit to allow her to ascend.

If nothing else, she should note that if Glinayeth and I have a child (unlikely since we are both rather old), she will carry Lorelei's name...assuming it's a girl. If it's a boy, we plan to call him Herman.

~Peapod

**Thanks for Reading**

If you enjoyed this book, would you please leave a review at the site you purchased it from? It doesn't have to be a book report… just a line or two would be fantastic and it would really help us out!

## *John P. Logsdon*
www.JohnPLogsdon.com

John was raised in the MD/VA/DC area. Growing up, John had a steady interest in writing stories, playing music, and tinkering with computers. He spent over 20 years working in the video games industry where he acted as designer and producer on many online games. He's written science fiction, fantasy, humor, and even books on game development. While he enjoys writing lighthearted adventures and wacky comedies most, he can't seem to turn down writing darker fiction. John lives with his wife, son, and Chihuahua.

## *Christopher P. Young*

Chris grew up in the Maryland suburbs. He spent the majority of his childhood reading and writing science fiction and learning the craft of storytelling. He worked as a designer and producer in the video games industry for a number of years as well as working in technology and admin services. He enjoys writing both serious and comedic science fiction and fantasy. Chris lives with his wife and an ever-growing population of critters.

*Crimson Myth Press* offers more books by this author as well as books from a few other hand-picked authors. From science fiction & fantasy to adventure & mystery, we bring the best stories for adults and kids alike.

Check out our complete book catalog:

www.CrimsonMyth.com